Wendy Douthwaite lives with her husband near Bristol where they run a book-selling business. She has written a number of pony stories including *The Orange Pony* and *The Christmas Pony*.

POLLY

Wendy Douthwaite

Illustrated by Joan Thompson

MACMILLAN
CHILDREN'S BOOKS

Summer Ponies first published 1989 by Macmillan Children's Books
under the title *Other People's Ponies*
Dream Pony first published 1990 by Macmillan Children's Books
under the title *All Because of Polly*
On Location first published 1995 by Macmillan Children's Books

This three-book edition published 2001 by Macmillan Children's Books
a division of Macmillan Publishers Limited
25 Eccleston Place, London SW1W 9NF
Basingstoke and Oxford
www.macmillan.com

Associated companies throughout the world

ISBN 0 330 48361 7

Text copyright © Wendy Douthwaite 1989, 1990, 1995
Illustrations copyright © Joan Thompson 1989, 1990, 1995

The right of Wendy Douthwaite to be identified as the
author of this work has been asserted by her in accordance
with the Copyright, Designs and Patents Act 1988.

1 3 5 7 9 8 6 4 2

A CIP catalogue record for this book is available from the British Library

Printed and bound in Great Britain by Mackays of Chatham plc, Kent

SUMMER
PONIES

One

"I'm sorry, Jess, it's out of the question."

"But, Dad— "

Across the supper table, Mr Caswell looked at his eldest daughter with eyes that were reproachful and even a little irritated, but when he spoke again his voice was quiet and understanding.

"Jess, you *know* I'm not saying this without having given the matter plenty of thought, but I have to tell you that we cannot afford to buy you a pony." He looked around the table, almost defiantly, at the four other members of the family.

They were unusually quiet. Everyone knew, including Dad, how desperately Jess wanted a pony, how the love of ponies and the longing for a pony of her own had become almost an obsession. Even Thomas, the youngest of the Caswell children, who was not quite four, had grown up with the idea that one day Jess would have a pony. He was constantly finding photographs of ponies in newspapers and magazines, which he would cut out carefully and bring to her, beaming with pleasure.

1

"There you are, Dess," he would say, not having yet managed the art of pronouncing the letter J, "p'raps that's your pony!"

When Dad had been promised promotion at work, the family had moved from the semi-detached house in Catley where they fitted tightly into three bedrooms and one living room. Jess had been filled with hope. The cottage at Edgecombe, twelve miles out into the country, seemed like paradise to all six members of the Caswell family. Four bedrooms and a boxroom meant that each of the three girls had a room of her own and Thomas, together with his clockwork train and soft toys, was accommodated snugly by the boxroom.

Jess had been sure that her dream was about to come true when Dad had taken them all to see Trumpeter Cottage, just two months ago, on a chilly February afternoon. They had stood in the frost-festooned front garden of the cottage, their breath forming small white clouds in the cold air. Thomas had chugged up and down the path, panting noisily and pretending to be a steam engine. In a voice that could not hide his excitement, Dad had told them that if Mum liked the cottage, too, then they could just about afford it.

The four Caswell children had followed their parents in a little straggly group, as they inspected the empty cottage. Eleven-year-old Jess, holding Tom's hand tightly, had been quiet, whilst inside her head she had repeated the words, Please let them buy it, oh, *please* let them buy it! For Jess had seen the small, rough-looking stable next to a stone shed, and the gate leading into an orchard. And Dad had looked at her, smiling, and nodding his head in the direction of the stable. *Surely*, it was all going to work out, and she would have her pony at last?

Clare and Kim, walking just behind her, talked in quick, excited whispery voices, and Jess knew that they had fallen under the spell of Trumpeter Cottage as she had. But would Mum love it? However, it did not take long to know how Mum felt. By the time they had reached the kitchen with its old range and long windows looking out over the back garden and beyond to one end of the orchard, Mum's eyes were shining. She sat in the deep window seat and looked across the room at Dad.

"We can do *so much* with this room," Mum said.

"The cottage will need a lot doing to it," Dad reminded her, trying to sound cautious, but not succeeding as he continued quickly, "but I can do most of it myself. The biggest job will be the plumbing, but that won't be too difficult – just time-consuming and perhaps a bit messy. The roof is sound and there's no damp. Most of the work will be decorating and fitting cupboards – things like that."

"I can do lots of that in the daytime, when you're at work," Mum put in, excitedly, "and the children will help, won't you?"

An excited babble followed, during which it was generally agreed that Trumpeter Cottage should and would belong to the Caswell family.

Now, as Jess sat in that same kitchen, staring down hard at her half-cleared plate and making an effort not to cry, she could not understand what was going wrong. Through the misery which hammered in her head, she heard Dad's voice explaining, and gradually the words seeped through. ". . . the promotion just hasn't come . . . the firm's going through a sticky patch . . . some of the others are even being made redundant—"

"Dad!" Jess looked up quickly, forgetting her own misery. "They're not going to make *you* redundant, are they?"

"No, it's all right, Jessie," Dad replied. "My job's safe enough as long as the firm stays in business." He looked round at them all again. "But I'm afraid it means no promotion for me just now, and that means that we'll have to be very careful not to over-spend." He looked at his wife. "I think they're all old enough to understand, don't you, Jan?" Mrs Caswell nodded, and he continued, "We all like it here, don't we?" He did not need to wait for a reply, but talked on, "Well, it was a much more expensive house to buy than our old one, and we do need to spend some money on it – and that means we can't buy luxuries. And ponies *are* luxuries. I'm sorry, Jess. Perhaps if things get better at work . . ."

Jess didn't cry that night as she lay in bed. It all seemed too important for crying. Moonlight streamed in through the half-open curtains, dimly lighting the square, cottagey bedroom which Jess was still not quite used to having as her own room. She looked at it with pleasure, her eyes wandering past the peeling paint on the thick, uneven walls, to the plentiful array of horse and pony posters which she had pinned up on her first day at the cottage.

On one wall of the room a deep recess held shelves, which Jess had filled with books and her ornaments – mostly of ponies. She gazed at the small figures sleepily. Sometimes she imagined her china ponies coming to life during the night and cantering about her room, leaping lightly on to the window sill, where they would snort and paw the wooden sill impatiently. The grey arab, which was her favourite, would poke his dainty nose in the air and whinny shrilly.

Jess felt her eyes closing as sleep gradually claimed her. She would think about her problem tomorrow. For now, the arab had grown to full size, and he was standing impatiently at the orchard gate, tossing his beautiful head and waiting for her to ride him . . .

Two

"It's awful!"

"What is?" Jess looked sideways at nine-year-old Clare, who sat next to her on the wall, swinging her legs to kick angrily at the stonework.

"Dad's saving money thing, of course," her sister replied, hunching her shoulders miserably. "He's going to let me keep on with my ballet lessons at school, but Mum said this morning that I can't keep up the extra Saturday morning ones."

Eight-year-old Kim looked up from the grassy bank below the wall, where she was sitting cross-legged, carefully making a daisy-chain. "Well, *I* was going to start having violin lessons next term and I can't now," she stated.

"Dad can't *help* it," Jess reminded them.

"'Course he can't," agreed Kim, stoically, "and Tom has had to stop going to play-school, so we're all in the same boat, aren't we?"

"But how am I going to become a famous ballet dancer, if I can't have lessons?" wailed Clare from her lofty position.

"Oh, Clare, don't be such a *pain*," Jess said, impatiently. "It doesn't help to moan. At least you're having *some* lessons."

7

Although offended by Jess's comment, Clare was silent. She remembered, suddenly, that Jess had been having a riding lesson once a week when they had lived at Catley, but since the move to Edgecombe she had not ridden at all.

Jess gazed meditatively across the lane to the field opposite, where a herd of young heifers grazed. "You know, I'm sure I could ride one of those, if I put my halter on it," she mused. Clare and Kim had given Jess a rope halter for Christmas. "I read about someone who rides her cows when they get too old for milking," Jess continued. "She had saddles for them, too!"

Kim looked up at her elder sister. "You wouldn't *really*, would you, Jess?" she asked, in awed tones.

"If I get desperate enough," Jess replied, grinning at her as she slid down from the wall. "Come on, here's the school bus!"

Kim had already made several friends in her class at their new school, and she disappeared into the crowded depths of the school bus when it pulled up alongside the three girls. Clare and Jess sat at the back. Clare had made one friend, who came to school on a different bus, but Jess, with her quiet and diffident ways, had found it difficult to make new friends. She discovered that everyone in the fourth form seemed to have at least one close friend and, although they were friendly enough, most of the time Jess found

8

herself sitting alone or wandering by herself in the playground at break times.

Today, she did not really mind too much, for she felt that she wanted to think hard about her knotty problem. How was she ever going to have a pony of her own – and indeed, how could she even find some way of riding? There seemed to be no riding stables close by at Edgecombe, and she couldn't ask Dad to drive her to Catley every week, just so that she could have an hour's ride – and anyway riding lessons were so expensive and . . . Jess, who had been wandering, head lowered, across the playground, came suddenly and painfully into contact with the tall wire fence at the edge of the playground.

"Ouch!"

"My goodness, you *were* deep in thought!" said an amused voice close by. Looking up, Jess saw that the speaker was Miss Claremont, her form teacher. Jess grinned sheepishly. She liked Miss Claremont, who was young and full of enthusiasm.

"Seems like quite a problem you're trying to work out," Miss Claremont continued, stepping a little nearer. Then she added, "Do you want any help – or is it private?"

"Well . . ." Jess hesitated. It would probably seem a silly sort of problem to a teacher. They tended to disapprove of passionate feelings about

9

ponies, she had found, for teachers felt that if you thought about ponies you wouldn't be thinking about your school work. Still, Miss Claremont seemed nice. She hesitated again, and then told her. As Miss Claremont listened, her eyes were surprisingly sympathetic, Jess thought, and when Jess had finished her story, Miss Claremont laughed delightedly.

"Well, you know," she said, "you just couldn't have told a better person than me because, you see, *I* love ponies too. I had one when I was young." Miss Claremont's eyes became dreamy. "He was a lovely little chestnut, with a white blaze and one white sock, and his name was—" She stopped suddenly. "Goodness, I mustn't ramble on like this."

"No, really, I don't mind," said Jess quickly. "He sounds lovely—"

"Yes, I know, but we were discussing your problem," interrupted Miss Claremont, "and I think I might be able to help you."

A loud clanging interrupted her. "Oh dear, there's the bell," she said. "We'll have to go in." Miss Claremont turned towards the staff room, saying hurriedly, "I'll see you here after lunch, Jess, and I might have some good news for you . . ."

The rest of the morning and lunchtime seemed interminable. Jess felt puzzled by Miss Claremont's words, and yet the teacher's voice had

10

sounded so optimistic. Jess just could not imagine what Miss Claremont had in mind. At last it was the lunchtime break, and Jess hurried out to meet the promiser of good tidings.

Miss Claremont was waiting in the same corner of the playground where they had met that morning, and Jess was surprised to see a girl from one of the other fourth-year classes with her.

Miss Claremont smiled warmly at Jess. "Oh good," she said, "you're here already. I've got to rush. Now, Jess, this is Rachel Fielding. She can tell you all about it. I'm due in the staff room for a meeting. 'Bye, both of you!" And in a moment she had vanished through the milling throngs of schoolchildren.

Rachel grinned at Jess. "Always on the go is Miss Claremont," she commented.

"She's nice, though, isn't she?" said Jess, feeling awkward and shy.

"Oh, yes, she's great," agreed Rachel. There was a small silence, then Rachel continued, "Well, I gather you've got a field and no pony?" Jess nodded. "Well," continued Rachel, cheerfully, "I've got a pony with no one to look after him for two months – so perhaps we should get together!"

"It's a temporary loan, you see, Dad. Rachel's father's a lecturer, and the whole family is going

11

to America for two months on an exchange. Rachel will have the pony shod before she goes, and he shouldn't really *cost* me anything. He won't need feeding, now it's April. And Rachel says if by any chance he's ill, I can put the vet's charges on their account. And he's *never* ill, anyway, she said. So, I *can*, can't I, Dad? *Please* say yes!"

Jess was breathless after her eloquent speech. Everyone turned towards Dad, who looked taken aback.

"You're all looking at me as if I were some sort of ogre!" he laughed. "Of *course* you can have him, Jess – you didn't really think I would say no, did you?"

All at once the kitchen was filled with noise, as everyone talked at once. Even Badger, the family dog, who was middle-aged and portly, raised himself up from beside the kitchen range and came over to see what was happening. He pushed his nose under Mum's hand and waved his tail, as if to say "Am I missing something?"

"What colour is he?" asked Mum, absently stroking Badger's black and white head.

Jess, pink with suppressed excitement, shrugged her shoulders. "I don't know," she admitted. "I didn't ask Rachel."

"How big is he?" asked practical Kim.

"About fourteen hands."

"What's he called?" Clare asked.

12

"Beetle." Everyone shrieked with laughter.

"Is he nice?" piped up Tom.

Jess looked a little doubtful. "I don't know," she said. "I hope so. Rachel just said that he was a bit of a handful. But I don't care," she added happily, "if he's only got three legs! I'm going to have a pony at last!"

Three

It wasn't exactly love at first sight. As Rachel led Beetle down the ramp from the horse-box, his ears were flattened firmly against his head and his eyes rolled menacingly. He hesitated at the top of the ramp, then careered down, dragging Rachel with him.

"He's quite strong," Rachel panted, when they reached firm ground. "There's a good old boy," she soothed, patting his neck, which rippled with muscles. "He *hates* horse-boxes," she explained to Jess. "Ouch! Stop it, Bee!" Beetle had stretched his neck to nip Rachel on the arm. She rubbed her arm, explaining with a wry smile, "He's always giving me these affectionate little nibbles – he doesn't realise they hurt!"

Rachel inclined her head towards the front of the horse-box. "All the gear's in the front," she told Jess. "If you get it out, you can have a ride – see what you think of him."

All at once, Jess became conscious of her family gathered around Beetle, and of Mr Fielding, who had driven the horse-box and who was now watching with interest.

"Er . . . perhaps it might be kinder to put him in his field," Jess suggested. "Let him get used to his new surroundings."

"OK," agreed Rachel cheerfully. "Perhaps you're right. He does get a bit uppity after a trip in the box. Come on then, Bee, old thing."

As Jess hurried off to collect the saddlery, she was aware of Rachel tugging at Beetle's head-collar, and of Beetle's stubborn, resisting stance. However, by the time she had returned, weighed down by the saddle, two bridles, a martingale, extra reins and bits, a halter and a bucket, she found that Rachel had persuaded Beetle to walk towards the orchard. Hurrying on ahead to store the saddlery in the shed, Jess then opened the orchard gate, and Beetle walked suspiciously into his new home.

The two girls, flanked by the various family members, watched Beetle from the gate as he wandered about the orchard, snatching a mouthful of grass here and there and sniffing and snorting, apprehensively.

"I hope you two get on together," Rachel said, quietly. "He's a stubborn old thing, is Beetle, but I love him."

Jess watched the sleek, dark bay pony as he wandered about the orchard. "Well," she replied with candour, "we can only try. But I'll look after him, I promise," she added, "and it *is* lovely to have him – a pony to ride at last!"

When everyone had gone, Jess made her way to the orchard again. It was late evening, and the sun was setting behind the old apple trees, casting long, crooked shadows across the grass. Beetle was quieter now, cropping the grass steadily in the open, treeless part of the orchard. Sitting on the top bar of the gate, Jess listened contentedly to the rhythmical munching, and watched Beetle's long black tail swishing. She daydreamed, imagining that Beetle was the grey arab. In her mind she saw him raise his head sharply, then throw it up and whinny loud and strong, before trotting over towards her with his high, flowing gait, halting beside her and pushing his soft nose into her hand. Beetle just raised his head slightly, peering at her without much interest before putting his head down again to get on with the important business of eating.

Never mind, Jess thought, back in the real world again, it's a start.

Jess leaned against one of the apple trees, exhausted, then slid her back down to sit dejectedly on the sun-warmed grass at its base. "I mustn't get annoyed," she told herself firmly, "that will mean that he's getting the better of me." She tightened her grip on the lead-rope as her inner feelings belied what she was telling herself. She *was* annoyed! He was just playing a game with her. Each time she approached him, holding out the carrot she had brought, whilst hiding the lead-rope behind her back, Beetle would walk nonchalantly away from her, watching her out of the corner of one eye. If she increased her pace, he increased his, and if she slowed down, so did Beetle. They had continued this exasperating game for nearly an hour. Jess had expected to be out on the lanes by now, but here she was still in the orchard with nothing but the lead-rope and an inquisitive robin to keep her company – and the back-end of Beetle, of course!

At a safe distance, Beetle cropped the grass placidly, keeping a wary eye on Jess in case she should begin again. He enjoyed this game, she could tell. He had played it many times before, obviously, and was a master at the art of evading being ridden. But she wouldn't be beaten! Resolutely, Jess stood up, ready to begin again. Beetle stopped munching and prepared to resume. Then both their attentions were diverted by a small figure, hurrying across the grass towards them, calling out,

"Dess! Dess! You forgot this!"

It was Tom, beaming his special little three-year-old beam, and staggering under the weight and bulk of Beetle's bucket.

"I put some grass in it," Tom confided, panting as he arrived at her side, " 'cos ponies *like* grass."

Jess rumpled his straight golden hair affectionately. He was so sweet sometimes! "Thanks,

Tommy," she said, gently, "but I don't think the bucket will—" As she spoke, a dark brown nose pushed down between them, towards the bucket. Quickly overcoming her surprise, Jess reached out and snapped the end of the lead-rope round the metal ring in the head-collar. At last she had him!

Jess hummed to herself as she brushed Beetle's already shining hindquarters. I must buy some pony nuts, she thought, as she brushed down towards his hocks. He's not going to think much of grass in his bucket every time – and the bucket's obviously the way to bribe him into being caught. Oh dear, she sighed, expense already! Seeing Beetle's hind leg raised ominously when she reached towards his tail to brush it, she decided that it looked all right as it was!

Leaving Beetle tied up outside the stable, munching at the hay-filled bag that Rachel had left – goodness! I'll have to buy a bale of hay, too! she thought – Jess fetched the saddle and bridle from the shed. Tom was her only watcher, sitting on the warm flagstones outside the shed, running his little metal cars through the earth between the stones, whilst emitting the appropriate car-engine noises.

"Are you going for a ride?" he asked.

"I hope so," Jess replied, hanging the bridle on a hook outside the stable. "But I can't be

19

sure of anything with *this* pony," she added, winking at Tom over the saddle. She lifted the saddle and rested it on Beetle's withers before sliding it down to its correct position on his back. Then, she reached under his belly for the end of the girth, which hung down on the other side. Beetle stopped munching and kicked upwards with one hind leg. Annoyed, Jess smacked him. "Stop it!" she commanded crossly. "You're very bad-mannered!" Beetle seemed surprised, and stood looking quite disconsolate, so Jess patted his neck, speaking more gently to him as he resumed his munching.

Having fastened the girth and pulled down the stirrup irons, Jess fetched the bridle from its hook and eyed the opposition carefully. There was no doubt about it – she was going to have to remove the head-collar before she could put on the bridle. Slipping the reins over Beetle's neck and holding them under his chin, Jess unbuckled the head-collar warily, waiting for Beetle to attempt to escape. But, much to her surprise, Beetle waited quite patiently while the bit was eased into his mouth and the headpiece pulled over his ears and settled into position. Jess buckled the throatlash, and they were ready to go.

"He doesn't seem to want to stand still," Tom pointed out, helpfully, from his playground on the flagstones, after Jess's fourth attempt at mounting Beetle.

"I can see that," muttered Jess through clenched teeth. Then in a sharp voice, she said, "Beetle! Stand *still* will you!"

He didn't exactly stand still, but there was a small moment without too much movement, during which Jess was able to jump into the saddle. As they trotted off down the drive, Jess found the stirrups and collected the reins.

" 'Bye, Tommy," she called. Then to Beetle, she said, "You really were badly brought up, you know."

Beetle merely snorted and cocked one ear back in Jess's direction, before testing her out with a large buck.

"Hah! I was ready for you!" Jess panted, triumphantly, as she again scrambled to regain the stirrups. She eased gently on the reins, slowing Beetle to a walk. "Now then," she continued, "we're going to walk for a while and then *I'm* going to decide when we trot!"

Four

Mum was out in the garden when Jess arrived back from the two-hour ride.

"How was he?" she asked, straightening up from weeding a flower border.

"Well, I'll say one thing for him," Jess commented, as she slid down from the saddle, "he's got character! Trouble is," she added, ruefully, "I can't quite decide what it is – bad or good!"

Mum strolled over to pat Beetle's sleek, dark neck. "He seems docile enough now," she said. "Ouch!" She backed away, rubbing her arm.

"Sorry, Mum, but that's one of his characteristics!"

However, Jess's spirits were high as she led Beetle towards the stable. It had been wonderful to be riding again, and a two-hour ride was luxurious! She had discovered on that first ride that Beetle was a difficult pony – moody and unpredictable. One minute he would be plodding sluggishly along the lane and the next he would be dancing sideways, acting like a two year old, having seen an imaginary piece of paper in the hedge. For some of the ride he had felt alert, his ears had been pricked and he had looked about him with interest. Then, suddenly, he would begin to plod, his ears would droop and when Jess leaned forward to talk to him, his expression was sour.

"What you need is a horse psychiatrist!" Jess told him, cheerily, as she removed the saddle. Beetle stretched out his neck and nipped her thigh.

"Ouch! You *horrible* pony!"

Jess leaned against his warm shoulder and considered Beetle thoughtfully. "You're not exactly *vicious*, Beetle," she told him, "you're just . . . crafty and underhand," she finished, laughing, as she unbuckled the bridle and took it off, replacing it with the head-collar. She patted him. "You're not *so* bad, really, are you, old boy. I begin to see what Rachel meant. And I do know *one* thing you like, don't I?" she added.

Jess had discovered, quite by accident, that Beetle had one passion. They had been trotting along a grass verge and had come to a drainage channel cut in the grass. Jess had expected Beetle to just trot over it, but he pricked his ears when he saw it, and took a tremendous leap over it, nearly unseating her. When she had turned him round to take him over it again, this time at a canter, his pleasure at jumping was evident. He had been in one of his plodding moods but, after the jump, he jogged along the lane, alert and lively and a pleasure to ride. Later on, up on the common, Jess had found a small jump that some other riders had built – just a small, rough brush fence. This jump was a source of delight to Beetle, who jumped it time and time again, giving a little buck of delight just before each take-off.

Now, as Jess closed the orchard gate, leaving Beetle cropping the grass, her mind was full of plans. Certainly Beetle was not a perfect pony, but Jess, who was wise beyond her years at times, did not expect perfection.

She looked at Beetle's shining hindquarters, watching his tail swishing rhythmically as he moved slowly away from her through the grass, and her heart was full of happiness. A field and a pony in it which she could ride – that was all Jess asked of life at present. Of course, her *own* pony would be wonderful but... Jess kept her mind on the attainable. Tomorrow, she would begin to build a jump in the orchard.

The letter from Rachel arrived on Monday morning, in the last week of term. The three Caswell sisters were late for the school bus.

"Come *on*, Jess. We'll miss it!" Clare called over her shoulder as she ran down the path, her school satchel bouncing on her back.

Kim paused in the doorway. "What are you doing, Jess? You know he won't wait!"

"I'm just seeing if there's anything for me," Jess replied, leafing through the letters which had dropped through the front door letter-box and lay scattered on the mat. "Ah! Here we are. Come on – race you!"

Still breathless, Jess read the letter in the school bus. Rachel's letter, written in large and untidy handwriting, was full of enthusiasm for America and the Americans.

"What does she say?" asked Clare from her seat next to Jess.

"She loves it," Jess replied, distractedly, as she struggled to decipher Rachel's erratic scrawl. After a pause, she added, "She's been to two barbecues."

Clare saw a new friend of hers at the front of the bus, and moved to a seat further up to talk to her, so Jess was able to settle down to her letter without interruption.

"How's dear old Bee?" Rachel's cheerful letter read. "I *do* miss him – difficult and awkward though he is. I forgot to tell you something about him – he *loves* jumping!" Jess smiled to herself, and then resumed her reading. "He can be quite good at it, too," Rachel's letter continued, "if he's in the mood! I usually enter him at Upper Edgecombe Horse Show at the Spring Bank Holiday in May, and since I won't be back, perhaps you'd like to have a go? I expect there'll be a poster about the show in the window at Edgecombe Post Office – there usually is."

Jess finished Rachel's letter, which continued to expound with enthusiasm upon the American way of life. Then she leaned back in her seat and daydreamed. She saw herself and Beetle flying over huge fences, watched by an admiring and cheering crowd. In a haze of contentment, Jess thought of nearly three weeks of holidays ahead, with Beetle to ride every day. Gradually, she became aware of a voice in her ear, and someone dug her in the ribs.

"I'm not *that* keen to get to school!" said the voice, accompanied by giggles from someone else, "but we're here!"

Awakened from her daydreams, Jess grinned sheepishly, and hurried to make her way down the bus.

Five

It was Mum who found the notice about Muffin.

On the first day of the Easter holidays – which turned out to be rather eventful – Jess was awake early. The sky was grey when she looked out of her bedroom window, but with a faint mistiness which promised sunshine later. Quickly pulling on jodhpurs and a shirt, Jess made her way down to the kitchen. Badger thumped his tail lazily from his bed by the old range. He raised his head to look at Jess with sleepily surprised eyes, before heaving a sigh and going back to sleep. Badger was a creature of habit, and six-thirty on an April morning was half an hour too early for him to think about waking up!

Jess filled the electric kettle and switched it on. She splashed her face with cold water at the sink. The bathroom upstairs was in the sort of chaos that can only get better, since Dad was busy at weekends and in the evenings, replumbing and decorating. For the present, the Caswell family had to manage with the only usable tap in the kitchen sink, or the old baby bath, filled with water from the kettle and taken upstairs for a "lick and promise" wash!

27

As Jess laid the tray with cups and saucers for tea to take upstairs, she looked out of the kitchen window. Behind the orchard, the sky glowed faintly pink as the sun rose, dispersing the mist. It was going to be a lovely day! Feeling that she must not waste a minute of these holidays – her first with her own pony to ride – Jess hastily made the tea. Well, maybe he wasn't quite her own pony, she reminded herself. However, she thought, philosophically, as she added the teapot, milk and biscuit tin to the tray, the best thing was to live for the present, and, for the present, Beetle, with all his faults, belonged to her!

Having surprised her parents with the tray of tea, Jess persuaded Badger to relinquish the comfort of his bed.

"You're getting much too fat and lazy," Jess told him sternly. Badger looked at her with the patient calm of middle age, and wagged his tail in agreement.

"I'll take you for a walk before breakfast," she told him. At the sound of the magic word, Badger bounced his fat form around the kitchen, as excited as a puppy.

"Poor old Badge," said Jess, fondly, "I've been neglecting you, haven't I, with all the excitement of moving and having a pony." She clipped on his lead. "Come on then – Keep Fit time!"

Outside the air was cool and crisp. The sound of birdsong was everywhere. Jess and

Badger visited Beetle in the orchard, and then began their walk down the quiet country lane.

"I'll let you off the lead when we get to the track," Jess promised – and then her heart stood still. Beside the road lay a small tabby cat, curled up just as though it were asleep. But Jess could see that it was not asleep; it was dead, probably hit by a car driven carelessly, maybe, and too fast through the night.

"Poor little thing," Jess sighed, looking down at the little tabby cat. It looked very thin and shabby. Maybe it had been a stray, Jess thought. It looked peaceful, curled up in the grass, so she left it there. A few yards further on, a grassy track meandered down to join the lane, and here Jess released Badger from his lead.

Bounding off, Badger was soon lost from sight, but Jess could hear his ample form crashing through the undergrowth. She grinned to herself – that would do him good! Jess wandered on, enjoying the walk along the grassy path. Then she became aware of Badger barking. It was not just an occasional bark – it was the determined, excited bark of a dog who has found something really interesting. Badger was part-retriever. What had he found now? Turning off the path, Jess followed the sound of the barking until she came to a small clearing. There was Badger, standing next to

29

an old tree stump, barking and wagging his tail, furiously.

"Badger, whatever have you – Oh!"

Looking down into the hollow part of the tree stump, Jess saw three tiny, wriggling creatures in a nest of bracken and dried grass. At first, she could not decide what they were, and then she realised – they were very young kittens. Immediately, Jess understood what must have happened. The little stray tabby cat had been looking after her three kittens in this quiet wood, and had been killed whilst out foraging for food. These three blind, wriggling lumps were orphans, and needed food and warmth urgently.

"Badger, you clever old boy," Jess said, patting him, "if you hadn't found them, they would have died." Picking up the kittens carefully, one by one, Jess transferred them to the bottom of her shirt, which she held in a cradle shape with her left hand. Two of the kittens meowed plaintively, but the third – the smallest – was quiet and hardly moved.

"We shall have to get you home quickly," Jess murmured. Obviously, this was the weakest of the litter and was already beginning to lose its strength.

Carrying the orphans carefully, Jess made her way back through the copse to the path, and then to the lane, accompanied by an attentive

Badger. He was very interested in these new acquisitions, and seemed to feel that they were his responsibility.

"You'd better stay with me," Jess told him. "I can't manage you on your lead *and* these three." But Badger was far too intrigued by the kittens to wander, and they all arrived home safely.

Dad was setting off for work when Jess and Badger reached the front door. He peered in at the contents of Jess's makeshift cradle and grinned at his eldest daughter. "We shall have to buy a bigger place, Jess, if you bring much more home," he chuckled. "I hope you manage to save them," he added, as he turned towards the garage, "that little ginger one looks as if it's on the way out."

Jess's heart twisted painfully. The smallest kitten mustn't die!

"Mum!" she called, "I've got something to show you!"

Mum assessed the situation quickly. Soon, the three kittens were in a cardboard box on top of the range, with some old sheeting packed around them, and Kim had been sent in search of dolls' feeding bottles. Although slightly ashamed of the fact, since she felt that she should have outgrown them by now, Kim still rather liked her dolls, and three usable feeding bottles were soon found.

"Here we are then, girls," said Mum, as she carefully poured warmed, diluted milk into the tiny bottles, "one each."

"I'll feed the little ginger one," said Jess quickly.

"Mm . . ." said Mum, "I'm not sure he's going to live, though, Jess."

Clare and Kim were soon able to feed the two tabbies, but the ginger kitten seemed uninterested in the doll's bottle that was presented to him.

"*Please* drink some," said Jess, anxiously, as the milk dribbled down past the kitten's mouth.

"I'll try opening his mouth," said Mum, "and you see if you can get some down him then. We'll have to force him, I'm afraid."

By this method they managed to persuade some milk to dribble down the ginger kitten's throat, but Mum looked doubtful. "They'll need feeding every couple of hours, I expect," she said, "but this one will need looking at every half an hour at first, I think, if we're going to save him."

"I'll look after him," Jess promised. "I'll set the timer!"

"All right," said Mum. "Come and have your breakfast. The kittens will be warm and comfortable on the range. I've got something to show *you*, now!"

Whilst Jess helped herself to cereal and milk and sat down next to Clare at the kitchen table, Mum fetched the local paper, which

had been delivered that morning. She turned to the middle pages and then handed the paper to Jess.

"There – what about that, Jess?" she asked, pointing to one of the small advertisements. Under the heading "Livestock", one of the items read, "Temporary home wanted for much-loved family pony while owner at college."

Jess looked up at her mother. "Do you think I could?" she said, excitedly.

"What is it?" asked Kim, through a mouthful of cornflakes.

"Someone wants a temporary home for a pony," Jess explained, her mind racing ahead. Beetle would be going home in six weeks' time – and how lovely, anyway, to have two ponies! But what about the cost of another pony? Jess frowned. "But maybe we can't afford it," she added, thoughtfully.

"Well, it wouldn't harm to telephone," Mum pointed out. "If the owner wants you to pay all the expenses, then perhaps we should think again."

"But you've *got* a pony, Dess," said Tommy, looking across the table at his sister with puzzled eyes.

"He'll have to go back to his owner in June," Jess explained. Then she turned to look at her sisters. "I could teach you two to ride!" she exclaimed.

Clare looked aghast. "You're not getting *me* on a pony," she declared emphatically. "I might get bow-legged, and then I couldn't be a famous ballet dancer!"

Kim giggled into her cornflakes. Jess, catching her eye, began to giggle, too, and Clare fled to her bedroom in tears.

"Now, girls, that wasn't very kind," Mum said mildly.

"But, Mum—" Kim began.

"I know," Mum broke in, "Clare takes everything in life too seriously. But that's just the way she is." Mum sighed. "Perhaps it won't harm her to be laughed at a little. She must learn not to take herself too seriously." She looked across the table at the two sisters. "But she *is* good at her ballet, you know," Mum told them. "Mrs Perkins, her ballet teacher, says that Clare is the best pupil she's ever had, and she thinks Clare could go on to do very well, maybe even make it her career."

Kim and Jess looked at each other and Jess pushed back her chair. "Perhaps we ought to go up to her," she said.

In her bedroom upstairs, Clare lay prostrate on the bed. She looked up with a tear-stained face when the other two came in.

"What do you want?" she sniffed.

Jess sat down on the bed. "We weren't laughing at *you*," she explained, diplomatically.

35

Kim joined in. "It was just the thought of you getting on a pony," she said, trying hard to stifle another giggle, "and then getting off with bent legs!" The giggle broke through, despite Kim's attempt to restrain it, and soon all three girls were laughing helplessly.

A shrill ringing stopped them.

"The timer!" Jess exclaimed. "It's time to feed the kitten again!"

Six

The rest of Jess's day was taken up with feeding the ginger kitten. Every half-hour, the kitchen timer rang shrilly and Jess managed to persuade a little more of the warm milk down the kitten's reluctant throat.

For the first time since he had arrived at Trumpeter Cottage, Beetle was not ridden. When Jess went to see him during the afternoon, he was standing disconsolately at the orchard gate. She only had time to give him a quick pat and to receive a nip on her shoulder, before she returned to the kitten.

At last, at teatime, the ginger kitten began to suck greedily at the doll's bottle, and Mum pronounced him able to be fed at two-hourly intervals.

When Dad came home from work, Jess showed him the newspaper advertisement.

"What do you think, Dad?"

"Jess, you know the problem just now."

"So you don't think I should?"

"Well, if it involves expense," Dad replied, "then I don't think we can consider it. But if the owners just want a home for their pony, and

37

they will pay the expenses, then that's fine." He leaned back in his chair and loosened his tie. "If you do go out to see it, I'm afraid I can't come. I *must* get on with that bathroom."

"I'll borrow Dad's car and take you," said Mum. "But go and telephone first, Jess. The pony might have a home by now."

Jess sat on the gate, watching her two temporary ponies as they grazed together in the orchard, and she could hardly believe her good fortune. Of course, it had all been due to Tommy, really. When the time had come to discuss the expense of keeping Muffin for the next year, Mrs Carter had gazed fondly at Tommy. He had smiled his angelic smile at her and she had been won over.

"Well, you know, Henry," she said, turning to her husband, "we did say the important thing would be that Muffin has a happy home." She turned to smile adoringly at Tommy. "And I'm sure these dear children will look after our little Muffin."

"You see," she confided, turning to Mrs Caswell, "Henry and I are getting on, now – Elizabeth came to us when we had quite given up hope of having a family. And now that she's going to Austria to stay with my sister for the summer, and then on to college in Switzerland, well, you see, we don't feel we can look after

Muffin. Elizabeth does it all, when she's here, and, to be honest, neither of us is very good with ponies."

"I know Jess will look after him, Mrs Carter, it's just the expense at the moment . . ."

"Oh, my dear, I quite understand," Mrs Carter interrupted, "but you needn't worry about that. We always buy Muffin's hay every year from the farm next door, so we'll have it sent over to you." She turned to Jess. "And when he needs shoeing, just tell Mr Croxford to send the bill to us – he's at Upper Edgecombe, you know."

And so it had all been arranged. The next morning, on his way to work, Dad had given Jess a lift over to the Carters' house, and she had ridden Muffin home.

Riding Muffin was a very different experience from being astride Beetle's broad back, as Jess soon discovered. To begin with, he was much smaller than Beetle. He was twelve hands high – too small for Jess, really, whereas Beetle was a little too big. But it was the different gait that Jess found so difficult to get used to. At the riding stable at Catley, Jess had been used to riding ponies of about Beetle's size, or slightly smaller, and she had grown used to the longer stride of a larger pony. As she bounced along on Muffin's back, rising to the trot at twice the normal rate, she wanted to laugh out loud. He was very sweet, though, she decided. His little ears were pricked and he held his head well, looking about him with interest. His long, thick, dark mane seemed to go all ways at once, falling on either side of his neck, and sticking up untidily between his ears. Despite his smallness, he was strongly built, and once Jess had learned to rise on every other stride of Muffin's trot, she began to enjoy riding the little chestnut pony.

Knowing Beetle's somewhat unpredictable nature, Jess had been a little concerned in case he did not take kindly to another pony sharing his orchard. However, she need not have worried. After a sniff and a squeal, the two ponies had settled down together quite amicably.

Now, Jess gazed thoughtfully at her two ponies. No – not *her* ponies, she reminded herself. She thought of her dream pony. Would he always remain a dream, she wondered. Her imagination conjured him up in the orchard at Trumpeter Cottage – her beautiful grey arab, with his banner tail and his exquisite, finely chiselled head. Always, when he saw her, he threw his nose in the air, tossed his long silken mane, whinnied that shrill call of welcome . . .

it's anything to do with the jumping." Again, he ran his hand slowly and carefully down the leg. "There's no swelling, and no heat." Straightening up, he gave Beetle a pat on the neck. "Just rest, I think, old fellow," he said. Turning to Jess, he added, "I'm afraid the show tomorrow is out. Sorry about that, but we can't take any chances, can we?"

So next morning it was Muffin who stood outside the stone stable whilst Jess, assisted by Tommy, groomed him thoroughly.

"That bit you've done is very good, Tommy," Jess encouraged.

Tommy beamed with pleasure as he paused in his grooming of one of Muffin's legs. The lower part of Muffin's shoulder was as far as Tommy could reach. "Mum's going to take us to the show after dinner," he told Jess.

"You'll enjoy that, Tommy – there'll be lots of other ponies there."

Doggedly, Tommy set to work again, while Jess fetched the tack. Jess was determined not to let her disappointment spoil the day. She and Muffin were going to have fun!

As Jess drifted off to sleep that night, she thought of the day at the show. Muffin had enjoyed himself immensely, and so had Jess. The noise and fun and excitement of the show had affected them both. Jess thought of the showground – horse-boxes and cars packing the field, the blare of loudspeakers, and the whinnies and grunts of ponies as they moved excitedly about the ground. She and Muffin had entered several gymkhana events, and had even managed to win a rosette in the trotting race, much to Jess's amazement. Muffin had out-trotted ponies much larger than himself to finish in third place in the final heat. Jess was sure that he had held his head higher after she had tied the rosette to his bridle.

But a happening in the day which had only lasted for a few minutes was still vivid and fresh in Jess's mind, and eclipsed all other thoughts. She and Muffin had arrived at the show at lunchtime, in plenty of time for the gymkhana events. The showing classes were still taking place, but most of them were over, and some of the ponies were being boxed. Even as Jess trotted Muffin up the lane towards the showground entrance, horse-boxes were lumbering out of the wide gateway and heading for home, their occupants having already competed in their classes.

Jess, conscious of her long legs astride such a small pony, walked Muffin next to the hedge, keeping away from the main body of the show. As they passed by a row of large and luxurious horse-boxes, Jess suddenly halted Muffin and gazed in fascination. It was him! It really *was* – her dream pony! As Jess watched, her legs dangling on either side of Muffin's fat stomach, her dream pony pranced across her path, head held high. A girl of about Jess's age led the pony, which tossed its beautiful arab head and whinnied excitedly.

"Hey! Polly – steady now," said the girl, smiling at the pony and reaching up to smooth its elegant dapple-grey neck. The pony pushed her beautiful nose against the girl's arm and danced excitedly beside her, like a beautiful silver leaf floating in the breeze, Jess thought. Jess was transfixed. The pony was even more beautiful than she had imagined. Its head was so finely moulded, she could have imagined that it was made of china. Its long, dark grey mane was fine and silky, and moved beautifully on the pony's elegant neck as it pranced. Jess watched in fascination as the pony was led up the ramp of one of the horse-boxes, its long banner tail swishing in the interior of the box as the girl lifted the ramp and fastened the bolts.

In a trance, Jess heard the engine start up – the driver must have been at the wheel already. The girl climbed into the passenger side of the Land-Rover which pulled the box, and the horse-box moved off, bouncing gently over the uneven ground. Slowly, but surely, her dream pony moved away across the field and out of Jess's life. As the end of the box disappeared from sight, Jess awoke from her soporific state, realising what an idiot she had been! Why, she asked herself crossly, as she and Muffin continued on their way, had she not *done* anything? Why hadn't she spoken to the girl – she had looked friendly enough. Jess's imagination took hold of her, as she saw herself talking to the girl, patting the dream pony's neck, and making an instant friend of the girl who then asked her back to tea. Here, Jess's imagination forgot Muffin's existence completely, as she stepped into the Land-Rover and travelled home with the girl, where she was offered a ride on the dream pony. It was as she jumped the four-foot gate, astride the beautiful arab, and watched admiringly by the girl, that Jess came back to earth with a bump – literally! Muffin, ambling along the grass path, ridden by a daydreamer who was paying him no attention, stopped suddenly and unexpectedly, and put his head down to graze. Jess found herself sliding down his neck to a sitting position next to his nose.

Muffin eyed her, mildly, and continued to pull at the grass. Just for a second, before she began to laugh, and as she looked up at the fat little pony, Jess felt an overwhelming sense of despair. Little Muffin was sweet, and Beetle was lovely, too, in his own way, but would she *ever* have her dream pony? Her desire for her own pony was as strong and as desperate as ever. She knew how lucky she was to be able to ride other people's ponies, but how she longed for one of her own – especially her dream pony. And she had seen him – or, more exactly, *her*. Her dream pony was called Polly – but she belonged to someone else. Jess heaved a large sigh of self-pity. All the ponies in the world seemed to belong to someone else . . .

"What are you doing *there*, Dess?"

Tommy, gazing down at her from his wide-open blue eyes, brought her sense of humour back to her.

"Being a hopeless rider!" Jess laughed, getting up and brushing herself down. Then Clare and Kim appeared, closely followed by Mum.

During the rest of the day, Jess's mind kept returning to Polly, the beautiful arab pony, but she tried hard to push these thoughts from her. Jess told herself, firmly, that her dream pony must remain as it had always been – a pony of her dreams. Reality was Muffin, tired but jogging happily home to his well-earned bucket of food.

It was when Muffin had been reunited with Beetle in the orchard, and Jess had taken herself wearily to bed, that she allowed herself to think again of the arab pony. After all, she *was* her dream pony, Jess thought. Through sleep-blurred eyes, Jess looked at her china horse and remembered Polly's beautiful china-like head, and the dark grey forelock which spread in wisps about

49

her large eyes. Was it her imagination, or did the china horse's head turn towards her? Polly and the china horse then merged into one beautiful grey arab pony which cantered through Jess's dreams that night.

Eight

The summer was long, glorious and very hot. Day after day, the sun shone from a cloudless sky. As the weeks and months passed, the green of the countryside paled and turned to brown. The orchard at Trumpeter Cottage became a lifeless desert, as the old apple trees searched out the last moisture from the ground.

Beetle's lameness had disappeared after a week's rest, and he had returned to Rachel in June. Soon, the grass in the orchard was non-existent, and Muffin stood forlornly in the dusty brown field. Much to Jess's relief, the promised hay arrived for Muffin in mid-July, and she began feeding him straight away. She rode round to see Mrs Carter to explain.

"I know he still looks well," Jess said, "but he's lost quite a lot of weight already and there just isn't any grass – he's really hungry!"

Mrs Carter stroked Muffin's neck gingerly. She was nervous of ponies and approached little Muffin with slight trepidation. "Of course you must feed him," she agreed. "You can't deny Muffin his food," she added, laughing. "It's the most important thing in life to him!"

51

As the summer progressed, restrictions were put on the use of water in the home, and the use of garden hoses and sprinklers was forbidden as the drought continued. The garden at Trumpeter Cottage, which Mum had tended so carefully throughout the spring, gradually shrivelled to a state of brown hibernation. Nothing grew, as some plants conserved energy, and others withered and died. The stream at the back of the cottage dried up, and Jess carried water to the orchard every day.

"It's typical!" said Dad one Saturday morning, pausing on his way through the kitchen, laden with pots of paint and brushes. "As soon as I finish the bathroom, we can't use it!"

Mum turned from the kitchen dresser. "Well, I did think that we might have a bath this evening," she suggested, tentatively.

"Can I have it first?" asked Kim, promptly.

"Oh, Mum, *that's* not fair," wailed Clare. "She had it first last time. I *hate* having someone else's bathwater!"

"Nobody *likes* having dirty bathwater," Kim retorted, "but if we're not supposed to use very much water, what else can we do? I don't really *want* a bath," she added, plaintively, to Mum.

"No arguing," said Mum, firmly. "It'll be Tommy first, anyway, since he goes to bed before the rest of you. We can't waste the water – at least one of you must use it after him." She sighed. "Oh, won't it be lovely when we have some rain . . ."

When it finally arrived, on the last day of the summer holidays, the rain came with a vengeance. All day, the sky darkened, and thunder rolled around the hills. At last, after tea, the first drops began to fall. The four Caswell children rushed out into the garden, followed by their parents.

"It's lovely! It's lovely!" Tommy cried, jumping up and down on the lifeless brown lawn, and holding out his chubby hands in an effort to catch the drops of rain as they fell. The girls, too, danced and shrieked with delight as the rain quickly soaked their hair and clothes.

"Come on in, you idiots!" laughed Mum, running back into the cottage. The rain was lashing down now, crackling against the dry, brittle leaves of the trees.

Jess stopped her dance of delight. "Look!" she panted, pointing towards the kitchen door. "Look at the kittens – they don't know what the rain is!"

Standing in line in the doorway, the two tabbies and Dandy were gazing out, wide-eyed. They crouched down, and Dandy hissed as the rain lashed down on the stone step and bounced off it into their faces. Jess ran back and picked up Dandy, hugging him. "It's rain, Dandy – real, lovely, wet rain!" she told him delightedly. "Now Muffin's water trough will fill up, and the flowers can grow again – and the grass!"

But Dandy was not too sure about it. For ten minutes, he and his two sisters sat by the kitchen stove, licking their paws and washing the strange wetness off their fur.

With the coming of the rain, the temperature dropped to autumn coolness. On the first day of term, Jess was quite glad to be wearing her new school winter clothes. It was strange to be putting on a skirt, socks and a blouse, after so many weeks of shorts and T-shirts, but Jess shivered in the unaccustomed chilliness of the September morning. Or maybe she was shivering with fright! Jess brushed her hair in front of the mirror in the bathroom, from where her own grey eyes looked back at her in trepidation. Goodness, she told herself, it was only a new school that she was going to – not a prison! It was such a large comprehensive – that was the trouble – and Jess would know very few people. Still, she reminded herself, Rachel would be there, somewhere, and there would be other faces she knew.

"Are you ready, Jess? We mustn't be late!" Dad called up the stairs, and soon the rush of getting away pushed all nervous thoughts from Jess's mind.

Kim, Clare and Tommy were still eating a leisurely breakfast in the kitchen, when Jess

54

rushed through the hall, gathering up her anorak and her school bag on the way.

" 'Bye, kids," Jess called, grinning in through the kitchen doorway at her younger siblings.

Clare looked mildly offended, whilst Kim wrinkled her nose. " 'Bye, big sister!" she mocked. "Don't get too lost in the big school!" Tommy turned his serious blue eyes towards Jess. "I'll look after Muffin for you," he stated importantly.

Jess laughed. "I *will* be coming home again, Tommy," she called, stopping to stroke Dandy, who had followed her downstairs and was balancing on the dresser, playing with the strap of her bag with his paw.

"Off you go!" commanded Mum, sweeping her out through the front door. "You don't want to be late on your first day." She smiled at her eldest daughter, knowing how nervous she was feeling. "Enjoy yourself, love, and don't worry – it'll take a while to get used to everything."

It was a dismal, grey morning. As Dad drove the car along the lane towards the motorway, he switched on the heater and the radio.

"We'll pretend it's still summer in here," he said, turning to smile at Jess. "This weather will take a bit of getting used to, after the lovely summer."

"Mmm." With time to think, Jess was beginning to worry again. While Dad hummed to the music

55

on the radio, Jess huddled nervously in her seat. They turned on to the motorway, and Dad switched on the car lights, since the sky had darkened and rain was falling steadily. Jess rubbed at the steamed-up window and peered out, watching the countryside flashing by.

It was then that she saw the pony. It was just a lightish shape, standing miserably by a gate, but something about it caught at Jess's heart. There was something wrong with that pony, she was sure. Jess rubbed the window again and strained to look, but pony, field and gate had sped by. Jess caught sight of a village near the motorway.

"What's that village called, Dad?" she asked.

"Oh – I think that's Currington Brayley," Dad replied.

"I didn't recognise it from the motorway." Jess's mind was busy working it out. The pony wasn't too far away from Trumpeter Cottage. The route to the motorway from the cottage curved round and away from the direction of the comprehensive school, so that after the car had joined the motorway, it had actually passed by the cottage and Edgecombe on the way. Currington Brayley was the next village along the valley after Lower Edgecombe, so the pony must be in a field somewhere between Lower Edgecombe and Currington Brayley.

Jess knew that she must find that pony. Even though she had only seen it for a short moment, she knew that something was wrong, although she could not explain to herself exactly what it was.

All through her day at the new school, Jess thought of the pony, and planned her visit. She saw Rachel, briefly, but only had time to hear about the visit to America and enquire after Beetle's lameness.

"Oh, I think he just decided to have a rest," Rachel laughed. "He was perfectly OK when he got home."

The day at the comprehensive school passed slowly, but was not as awe-inspiring as Jess had anticipated. She even found that some other members of her year felt as nervous as she did in this new and much larger environment. At the end of the school day, Jess caught the bus home. She sat restlessly in the bus as it slowly rattled its way around the twisting country lanes. The driver seemed to be in no great hurry, and he chatted cheerfully to each new passenger who arrived. At last, the bus eased to a halt by the ancient oak tree at Edgecombe Post Office.

"Enjoy your first day?" asked the driver, as Jess dismounted.

Jess smiled. Everyone knew everything about everyone else in the country! "Yes thanks," she replied.

The rain had stopped during the afternoon, but the sky was still overcast. Jess hurried up the lane to Trumpeter Cottage. Sitting on the gatepost, his tail curving round the post, was Dandy. He meowed his greeting when he saw Jess, and climbed into her arms to be cuddled when she reached the gate.

"Hello, little Dandy," she crooned, "have you missed me?" On her way up the path, Jess told Dandy about the pony, and she told Mum, too, as she hurried upstairs to change. There was Muffin to see, and Tommy, who followed her, questioning her constantly about the day at school, but at last Jess was away astride her bicycle.

It wasn't too difficult to work out approximately where the pony's field was situated. Within twenty minutes, Jess was in the area, and then followed a field-by-field search. At the fourth gate, Jess stopped, dispirited. Surely, she hadn't made a mistake? Perhaps the pony had been taken away . . . But no, there it was! As Jess stared again at the pony, this time from a closer proximity, her heart turned over – and then over again! Not only did the pony look miserable, neglected and in trouble, but also, unless Jess was very much mistaken, it was her dream pony – Polly, the beautiful grey arab!

Nine

"Polly! Hello, Polly!" Jess called, and the pony turned her head wearily. Climbing the gate, Jess approached the pony. Tears stung her eyes as she remembered the beautiful pony that had danced across her path at Upper Edgecombe Horse Show. Jess remembered how she had thought, then, that Polly seemed like a beautiful silver leaf, dancing in the wind. Her heart ached, now, when she saw how wearily Polly moved, and how dull were the large, dark eyes which turned to look at her as she approached. The pony's fine coat, still wet from the day's rain, clung to her body, accentuating her thinness. Jess noticed how awkwardly Polly was standing next to the water trough. As she came closer to the pony, she could see the reason.

Over a period of months, Polly's hooves had grown, and her shoes, firmly and well fitted by the blacksmith, had stayed in position. As a result, the growing feet had split, and formed into awkward shapes, restricted as they were by the farrier's nails and the iron shoes. Polly was now only able to move about awkwardly and painfully.

The ache in Jess's heart turned to anger. How *could* the girl who owned this beautiful pony have treated her in this way? It was obvious from looking at the state of the field, and at Polly's thinness, that she had not been fed during the drought. Hot tears of anger and frustration fell on Jess's cheeks. What could she *do*? Running back to her bicycle, Jess pulled out the bag of carrots she had brought, and hurried over to give them to the pony, who crunched them up greedily. Jess thought quickly. She must cycle home and return before dark with as much hay as she could manage on her bike – or maybe Mum would give her a lift in the car. Then, she must find out where the girl who owned Polly lived, and tell her of the arab pony's distress. Again, anger welled up inside Jess as she thought of the needless suffering that Polly was enduring, through her owner's thoughtlessness. And yet, Jess thought, the girl she had seen had not seemed like that. She had appeared to love Polly . . . it was puzzling.

Her mind full of these thoughts, Jess allowed herself a moment to smooth the dappled neck and to whisper in one of Polly's small, pointed ears, "I'll be back, girlie – don't you worry. You shall have some food soon." She imagined that she could see a spark of hope in those dark, liquid eyes. As she reached up to give Polly a final pat, a voice called out:

"I say!"

Jess swung round to see a man and a woman standing by the gate. The man waved a hand and called out again.

"Do you think you could just check the water in the trough for us, please? It would save us coming through the mud."

Casting a cursory glance in the direction of the trough, which contained a plentiful supply of water, Jess left Polly and walked across to the gate. They must be her parents, she thought, seething with anger. She can't be bothered to come herself, and they're too lazy to walk across the field!

Jess reached the gate. "There is plenty of water," she told them coldly. She took a breath, ready to tell them, urgently, how cruelly and thoughtlessly the pony had been treated – but the woman spoke first.

"Thank you *so* much, dear." She smiled at Jess, but her eyes looked worn out and defeated. Jess hesitated, and the woman continued. "We are in a hurry, you see, to visit our daughter. She's in hospital – we just came to see that her pony is all right. We have checked her water all through the drought, but now I expect, with the rain, we shan't have to come."

All at once, Jess understood, and her anger vanished.

"Oh . . . oh, I see . . . I'm sorry," she stammered. Then she spoke again, the words pouring

61

out and tumbling over each other. "But, you see, your daughter's pony *isn't* all right. She's starving. And her feet are in a terrible state – she can hardly walk. She needs food and a blacksmith – urgently!"

The two stared at Jess blankly, and Jess had the feeling that this was just one more problem to add to their already problem-strewn life. "But . . . but, we had no idea—" the man began.

"It's all right," Jess said, quickly, "please don't worry. I can help – if you'd like me to. I've got some hay at home. I can bring her some. But she really *does* need the blacksmith. I think she's very uncomfortable – her feet are in a bad state."

The man turned to his wife. "But this is terrible, Maisie," he said to her. "Beckie thinks we are looking after her pony – but we seem to have neglected it, without realising." He turned back towards Jess. "We would be very grateful, young lady, if you *could* help," he told her, quietly. "Should we have fed the pony – in the *summer*?"

Jess nodded. "There's been no grass," she explained, "and now there will be just mud for a while."

"How stupid of us," the woman contributed. "We thought that water was the only thing to worry about in the drought, you see . . . and the blacksmith – well, Beckie always sees to that . . ."

The man looked at his watch, "Now, look – er, I'm afraid we don't know your name—"

"Jess Caswell – I live at Edgecombe, in Trumpeter Cottage, just down the lane from Edgecombe Farm."

"Well, Jess, if you could help us, we would be most grateful. We have to go to the hospital now." His eyes clouded with pain as he explained. "She's very ill, you see, so we must go. If you *could* give the pony some hay, and arrange for the blacksmith to come, we will call round to see you – you mustn't be out of pocket." He shook her hand. "Thank you very much, Jess. We'll see you again – oh, by the way, we live at Horwood House in Currington Brayley – Stockwood's the name."

That night, Jess lay in bed, unable to sleep. Questions and thoughts kept forming in her mind. How was Polly now, in her muddy, grassless field by the motorway? Would the blacksmith be able to come tomorrow? After she had taken some hay to Polly in her field, Jess had left a message with the blacksmith's wife, explaining the urgency, and asking if he could possibly call at the field on the following evening, after schooltime.

Then Jess's mind turned to the Stockwoods. How ill was Beckie Stockwood, she wondered sleepily, remembering the girl who had smiled up at her beautiful arab pony with such delight at the horse show. As she drifted off to sleep, Jess's last question was would Mr and Mrs Stockwood let her look after Polly while their daughter was ill? There was room in the orchard with Muffin. And, maybe, when Polly's feet had been attended to and when, with some food inside her, she had picked up, maybe . . . just maybe, they would let Jess ride her . . .

Jess yawned, stretching down her hand to stroke Dandy, who was curled in a tight ball on the duvet, next to her legs. Sleepily, Dandy opened his yellow eyes and purred.

"That would be so lovely, Dandy," Jess murmured, already half asleep, "to ride Polly . . ."

Ten

"Well, I don't know, I'm sure!"

Stan Croxford, the blacksmith from Upper Edgecombe, looked askance at Jess as he lifted out his portable anvil from a battered old van, and then reached in again for the butane burner. He straightened up and looked at Jess, thoughtfully.

"I don't know what your secret is, Jess Caswell, but today was the *third* time in less than six months that I've been telephoned by an owner, saying that *he* will pay for the shoeing of a pony that *you* are looking after!"

"I'm only helping out with this one," Jess admitted, smoothing Polly's thin neck, "but I'd love to look after her properly."

Again, Stan Croxford reached into his elderly vehicle, this time producing a bag of tools. "Is that so?" he said, grinning. "Well, Mr Stockwood gave me to understand that you might be looking after Polly for a while – said any attention needed would be paid for by him."

Jess held Polly, while Stan lifted the pony's front foot and began pulling out the nails in the old shoe. "What I'd *really* like," Jess confided, "is to keep her in the orchard at the cottage, with Muffin – you know, the pony you shod last month—"

"I know," Stan chuckled, "another one!" Carefully, he trimmed Polly's broken hoof. "You specialise in other people's ponies, do you?" he asked, releasing his hold on the hoof and straightening up again.

"I'm afraid so," Jess admitted, sadly.

"Never had one of your own?"

She shook her head.

Stan moved round to the other front leg. "Never mind," he said cheerily. "You'll have it one day – if you really want one. I was twenty-four before I had my old Major . . ."

For the next three-quarters of an hour, Jess listened to Stan Croxford's adventures with his sixteen-hand cob, whilst inside her mind an excited hope tingled. Would she, perhaps, be allowed to look after this beautiful pony?

While her feet were cut back to shape and new shoes were fitted, Polly stood, pulling at the hay in a net which Jess had brought over on her bike.

"There we are, then," said Stan, at last, stepping back to admire his work. "That's a good job, if I do say it myself. You look much more comfortable now, Polly," he told the arab pony. "A bit of food inside her – pony nuts and such like," he said, turning to Jess, "and she'll be as right as rain in no time. Surprising how

hardy these arabs are, you know, despite their light build."

Jess leaned on the gate, watching Polly pull at the hay, and admiring the light build that Stan had referred to. Of course, Polly was very thin now, but after some feeding . . .

The sound of a vehicle coming to a halt in the lane disturbed Jess's thoughts. She turned to see the front end of a Land-Rover. Emerging from the doors were Mr and Mrs Stockwood and then, much to Jess's surprise, her father appeared on the scene.

"Dad! Whatever are *you* doing here?"

He grinned at her. "Any excuse to get out of the decorating," he said, winking.

"Jess, we've come to ask you a favour," said Mr Stockwood. "Your parents say that they don't mind and they think that you won't, either."

Jess looked at him with a puzzled expression on her face. Then Mrs Stockwood stepped forward.

"Jess, dear, would you do us a big favour – would you look after Polly at your home, while Beckie is in hospital? Keep her in your orchard and feed her – ride her if you would like to." She paused. "*Please*, Jess, it will be such a relief to us to know that she is being looked after."

Jess gazed at them in amazement. She heard Stan Croxford chuckling as he loaded the equipment into his van.

At last, Jess found her voice. "*Like* to?" she questioned, incredulously, "but I'd *love* to!"

At Trumpeter Cottage, Jess felt as though she were part of one of her own dreams, as she led Polly down the ramp of the horse-box into the lane. With comfortable shoes fitted and some hay inside her, Polly seemed to have regained some of her former spirit. She viewed her new surroundings with interest, tossing her beautiful head and even jogging on the spot beside Jess.

"She's beautiful, isn't she?" said Mum, who had come out to see the new arrival, accompanied by the rest of the family, including Badger and the three kittens. Muffin, hearing the sound of Polly's shoes clattering on the road, whinnied from the orchard, and received a return call from Polly.

"What a large family you have!" laughed Mrs Stockwood. "I'm sure Polly will like it here."

Still feeling slightly unreal, Jess led Polly down the drive, past the old stone stable to the orchard, where a very curious Muffin was waiting at the gate.

Later on, after a quick tea, Jess sat on the orchard gate, watching the two ponies eating their hay from the net, which Jess had hung from one of the old apple trees. Watching Polly's grey shape soften into the dusk, Jess remembered Stan Croxford's words: "You specialise in other people's ponies, do you?" he had asked.

Jess sighed. Never mind, she thought, as Polly turned her head to gaze at Jess out of the darkness, just for now, at least, my dream pony really *is* here in the orchard!

"Polly," she called, softly, and out of the dark came a gentle answering whicker. Then the back door of Trumpeter Cottage opened, throwing out light on to the path.

"Jess!" Mum called, "are you coming in, or shall I bring out a tent for you!"

Jess slid down from the gate. "Goodnight – other people's ponies," she called, but this time her only reply was the steady munching of hay from the night-filled orchard.

Eleven

Mr Warburton, the vet, came over to Trumpeter Cottage to give Polly a check-up, having been sent by Mr Stockwood.

"Basically, she's reasonably fit," he confirmed cheerfully. "Lucky you caught her in time, though," he added. "She just needs nutrition." He took a syringe from his bag. "I'll give her a vitamin injection," he told Jess, "and I'll give you some powder to mix in her food."

That afternoon, a delivery of pony nuts, crushed oats, bran and flaked maize arrived from the Corn Stores in Currington Brayley.

"All paid for by Mr Stockwood of Horwood House," the delivery man said, as he carried each sack down the path of Trumpeter Cottage, and deposited it in the stone shed next to the stable. "I've arranged for some hay and straw to be sent over to you early next week," he added.

After the delivery van had driven away, creaking carefully around the curving lane, Jess gazed thoughtfully at the bulging hessian sacks. In true cat fashion, the three kittens were investigating these new arrivals. Dandy, always the leader, was

71

the first to climb one of the sacks, and survey the world of the shed from its top.

Jess began feeding Polly straight away, giving her a small feed twice a day, to begin with, as instructed by the vet, and she continued to put out hay for both the ponies. After only a week, the difference in the grey arab was noticeable, and at the weekend Jess decided to ride Polly for the first time.

"I'll ride you this afternoon," Jess promised Muffin, who stood disconsolately at the gate, as Jess led Polly towards the stable. The grey pony danced beside her excitedly.

"You know you're going for a ride, don't you?" Jess said, as she brushed Polly lightly. All that week, Jess had groomed the grey mare thoroughly, each evening after school, and now her coat shone like silk.

"I wonder when you were ridden last," Jess mused. "Perhaps it was the show at Upper Edgecombe." As she saddled the grey arab, Jess found herself thinking about Beckie Stockwood. What had happened to her, she wondered, and how was she now? How long would it be before she could ride again?

"You know, Polly," Jess said, as she tightened the girth, "I think I'll write to her."

Jess found her hands trembling with excitement as she gathered up the reins and prepared to mount. She could feel excitement tingling through Polly, too. Jess jumped into the saddle and at last she was astride her beautiful dream pony! Feeling again as though she were back in one of her dreams, Jess felt Polly's light, quick movements as they started off down the path and into the lane.

"She feels wonderful!"

Jess's eyes shone as she described her first ride on Polly to Clare and Kim.

"She must feel terribly different from Muffin," Clare observed. Clare sat on one side of the fireplace, drawing the kittens, who were asleep on the rug, whilst Kim sat cross-legged on the other side, frowning and chewing her pencil over her English homework.

Trumpeter Cottage boasted a large lounge, but invariably the family congregated either in the big, square kitchen, warmed by the old range, or – where the girls now were – in the cosy living room, which led from the kitchen and which also served as a dining room. When not in use, the dining table was pushed against the window, and the big, comfortable chairs formed a semi-circle in front of the fire.

A standard lamp and the bright log fire lit the room, and purple shadows danced and fell on the walls at the whim of the flames. Outside, on this particular night, the weather was wild, wet and windy. An easterly wind shook the windows, and tugged at the ivy which grew over the outside walls, lifting it and throwing it back, so that the long tendrils scratched and tapped against the window panes like the claws of some large and desperate animal.

"She's gorgeous," Jess told Clare dreamily. "It's like riding on a cloud – she's so light and . . . sort of . . . delicate."

Kim looked up. "I wish *you* could write my composition homework," she said, plaintively. "I'm just no good at English – I've got to write about 'A sunny day at the weekend'."

"Well, that's easy," Jess replied, "I'll describe what it's like going for a ride on Polly and you can write it down. After all, it doesn't say it has to be about what *you* do." Kim looked doubtful.

"You can add some bits about you, too," Jess encouraged, warming to the idea, "then it will be your own work. It's not cheating – just getting a helping hand! I'm going to write to Beckie, anyway, and I'll describe riding Polly to her."

"Who's Beckie?"

"Beckie Stockwood. She's the girl who owns Polly. She must feel terribly fed up with not being able to ride. I thought it might cheer her up."

Jess posted the letter the next day, addressing it to Horwood House, and enclosing with it a drawing of the kittens asleep by the fire, and another one of Polly's head. Towards the end of the following week, a letter arrived for Jess, postmarked from Bristol. It was evening before Jess received it, since she had to leave for school each morning before the post arrived.

Hanging her anorak in the hall, and extracting a piece of chocolate cake from the tin in the kitchen, Jess made her way to the living room, opening the letter as she went. Clare and Kim were already ensconced in their favourite places by the fire. Clare was reading and Kim sighing over her homework.

"Not English again?" Jess mumbled, through the chocolate cake.

"No, Maths this time," Kim replied, glumly. Looking up, she added, more cheerfully, "I got an A for the composition about you and Polly." She grinned up at Jess, "Mrs Bloxton said I'd made a dramatic improvement!"

"Mm . . ." Jess was lost to all thoughts of Kim's miraculous change with her English work, as she read the long letter from Beckie Stockwood.

"Dear Jess," the letter began. "It was lovely to receive your letter last week. Sorry I've been so long in replying, but I have had pneumonia, following an operation, and I didn't feel much like writing – or doing anything! Actually, I can't remember much about the last two weeks – I think I was quite ill and Mum and Dad were worried. Anyway, I'm better now, and they have

75

told me all about you. Thank you, *thank you* for looking after Polly for me . . ."

Jess sat cross-legged on the hearth-rug next to the kittens, and leaned against one of the armchairs as she continued to read the letter. Beckie told of the car accident which had sent her into hospital in Bristol as an emergency. It had been in June when the accident happened. Beckie had been driven by her mother to the outskirts of Bristol for her weekly flute lesson. On the way home, another car had driven through the traffic lights at a junction, crashing into their car on Beckie's side. Mrs Stockwood had received only minor cuts and bruises, but Beckie had been rushed to hospital.

"I can't remember anything about that day," Beckie wrote, "or for quite a time afterwards. And since then I seem to have had nothing but operations. Still, things are looking a little more hopeful now. The nurses are even talking about 'when you go home'! I don't think it will be for quite a while, though, so I *really* am grateful to you – especially for discovering Polly's condition when you did. I kept asking Mum and Dad if she was all right, and of course they thought all they had to worry about was water, with the drought we've had. Never mind, it's all water under the bridge – if you'll pardon the pun!"

The letter was cheerful and optimistic, and finished, "Please, *please* do write again. It was so

lovely to hear about Polly. Please tell me about you, too – and your family and pets. I've got no brothers or sisters, and only Polly as a pet, so I'm rather boring! Still, Polly makes up for everything – she's such a sweet pony, isn't she? I love the drawings you sent. I miss Polly so much – I can't wait to get home and ride her. Perhaps we could ride together? *Please* write. Love, Beckie.
PS Enclosed is a drawing of the garden here. It's not a very exciting subject, but there's not much else to draw except the other patients – and the nurses, of course, but *they* don't stay still for long enough! It was a nice day today, so the nurses let me sit outside."

"Gosh, *that's* good," Kim exclaimed as Jess held the drawing up for inspection. "Did Beckie do it?"

Twelve

Letters began to fly back and forth between Trumpeter Cottage and the hospital in Bristol. Sometimes Mr and Mrs Stockwood arrived at the cottage, bearing Beckie's fat envelope.

"You're working wonders," Mrs Stockwood told Jess, on one of their visits. "Beckie has improved such a lot since you began writing to her. She was getting depressed with being in hospital for so long – thought she'd *never* come out!"

"Well, we began to think so, too, didn't we, Maisie?" Mr Stockwood contributed.

"That's right. But now they say it won't be long before she will be home!"

Jess noticed that Mrs Stockwood's eyes had lost the strained, almost defeated look which she had observed when she first met Beckie's parents. Her eyes smiled at Jess, now, as she rested a hand on her shoulder.

"You've no idea how grateful we are, Jess," Mrs Stockwood told her.

"But . . . but, I haven't done anything," Jess insisted. "It's wonderful being able to look after Polly – and I really enjoy writing to Beckie and getting her letters. We seem to . . . to, well, *think* the same about things . . ." Jess stopped, feeling suddenly embarrassed. She picked up Dandy and stroked him to hide her confusion.

"Well, you've taken a load off our minds, young lady, one way and another," said Mr Stockwood, in his deep, no-nonsense voice. "Our Beckie's a different girl since you came along."

Mum handed round tea and biscuits, and Jess was able to slip away to read Beckie's latest letter in the solitude of her bedroom. The letter was full of excitement.

"Doctor James has said that I'll be home for Christmas," Beckie wrote. "Won't that be wonderful! I seem to have been in here for ever!"

With each of Beckie's letters was enclosed a drawing, sometimes two. This time, it was a drawing of Sister Pye – "Old Crusty" as the nurses called her. "Actually," Beckie wrote, "she's very kind, but she doesn't like to show it. She struts around the ward all stiff and starchy, with her lips pursed, watching the nurses and pouncing on them if she thinks they're doing something wrong. But she's really great if you're in pain, or feeling miserable."

Jess paused in her reading. Beckie's letters were always cheerful. She didn't ever mention that she felt miserable, or depressed, but she must do . . .

"It's October now," the letter continued. "Just think, Jess, I might be home in two months – eight weeks! Oh, I'm getting excited already!"

Jess leaned back against the headboard of her bed and tried to imagine what it must be like to be in hospital and longing to be home with Polly. She looked out through her window and across to the orchard. She could just see two swishing tails – one black and one dark grey. She sighed. She must remember that her beautiful dream pony belonged to someone else and soon Polly must return to Beckie, who loved her. It was hard to have found your dream pony and then to know that she could never be yours . . .

Dandy had followed Jess upstairs. He jumped up on to the bed and rubbed himself against her, purring and kneading the duvet cover with his small ginger paws. Jess gathered him into her arms and hugged him.

"Never mind, Dandy. I've got you, haven't I?" Dandy's purrs grew even louder and his yellow eyes gazed adoringly at Jess. "Come on," said Jess, "let's go and see Polly. If I'm quick, I can ride to the woods and back before dark."

The evenings were drawing in. Next week, the clocks would go back, and there would be no time after school in which to ride. But if she got up early, perhaps she could ride in the extra hour . . . Her depression forgotten – or perhaps pushed to the back of her mind – Jess ran down the narrow cottagey stairs, two at a time, followed by Dandy, who skittered excitedly down the stairway, imagining intriguing animals to pounce upon at every turn.

The weeks seemed to fly by. As each day passed, Jess could not help thinking that it was another day less with Polly. She tried hard not to think about it, sharing her precious riding time between the two ponies. The steady flow of letters to and from Beckie continued. As October gave way to November, and then December arrived, Jess knew that the time was approaching when she must relinquish her part in Polly's care.

"But I'll always love you, Polly," she told the grey mare after school one evening in early December. "Beckie will let me come over to see you and ride you sometimes – she said so."

Jess heard the unmistakable sound of Tommy approaching through the dusk. Tommy's passion for ponies – and Muffin in particular – had increased over the months. Everywhere he went, he would click his tongue in an imitation of the sound of horses' hooves. When enquiries were made, he would explain that he was riding Muffin.

Mum was still insistent that Tommy was too young to ride. "You'll have to give in, Mum," Jess had told her that week, "to save his sanity!"

"But he's only four, Jess."

"Mum, lots of four year olds ride!"

Now, Tommy arrived, breathlessly tongue-clicking, at Jess's side.

"You can't be riding Muffin, Tommy," Jess informed him. "Muffin's there, in the orchard, eating his hay."

"'Course I'm not, silly," Tommy replied stoutly. "I'm riding Miffin!"

"And what's Miffin like?" Jess enquired, laughing.

"He's just like Muffin," Tommy stated unabashed. "He's his twin brother!"

Thirteen

The day had come at last. Jess had known that it must. She had expected to feel miserable at the prospect of losing Polly, and excited at the thought of meeting Beckie. But, somehow, she did not seem to feel *anything*.

It was Saturday. A pale sun shone in a cloudless sky, and the air was cold and crisp – one of those December days that are perfect for riding. But, for Jess, it might as well have been pouring with rain, for she could not enjoy the ride to Horwood House, a distance of about four miles along the beautiful Edgecombe Valley.

No member of the Caswell family had been able to extract many words from Jess that morning. She munched her way mechanically through her bowl of muesli, while Tommy chattered to her about Muffin. Eventually, even Tommy's cheery voice came to a faltering halt. At last, when Jess had groomed and saddled Polly, lingering over these chores for longer than usual, a subdued family gathered at the gate to say goodbye to Polly.

"I'm sure we shall see you again, Polly," said Mum, trying to sound cheerful. She smoothed the arab's silky, grey neck. Polly pushed her soft nose hopefully into Mum's hand and was not disappointed. As Polly crunched her carrot, Clare and Kim patted her. Tommy, standing a little apart, was unusually quiet.

"Aren't you going to say goodbye to Polly, Tom?" Dad asked. Tommy shook his head, his grey eyes brimming with tears. Tommy, although bright and cheerful, was very sensitive.

"I think I'd better go," Jess muttered. She squeezed Polly with her heels and the pony stepped away with her usual willingness. Soon, they were away from the cottage, swinging down the lane towards Currington Brayley.

Jess was quiet during the ride. Normally, she would chatter to Polly, watching those neat little arab ears flicking back to listen, and delighting in the lightness of Polly's step. But today a cloud of gloom had settled over Jess, leaving her feeling numb and empty, and she was glad when the village of Currington Brayley came into sight.

Beckie had sent instructions for how to find Horwood House, and had even drawn a map. Jess had looked at it so many times, and read the instructions over and over, that she knew the way by heart. Turn left at the first cross-roads after the 30-mile-an-hour sign, past the church, then second right. Horwood House was down the lane, just past Horwood Farm.

Jess and Polly had to wait whilst a herd of Friesian cows pattered across the road from the farm, and into the field opposite. A border collie darted from side to side, busily ensuring that his herd would not stray. Not that they looked in any danger of straying, Jess thought, as she watched the patient cows plodding slowly across the lane, lowered head to swishing tail. One cow *did* stop to stare. Her sisters kept swaying past – a gently flowing black and white river continuing on its way across the lane. The rebel cow turned large, curious eyes upon the newcomers.

Polly suddenly remembered her arab ancestry, and tossed her head and pointed her nose in the air. She whinnied shrilly and pawed the ground, then pranced and danced across the lane in mock fear. For the first time that morning, Jess laughed.

"You idiot!" she chuckled, stroking Polly's neck soothingly. "You're not a bit frightened, really – and you know it!"

The collie, full of importance, hurried to direct the cow, making the way clear for Jess and Polly to move on down the lane towards the gates of Horwood House.

Here it was, then! As Jess viewed the elegant, old, ivy-clad house, noting the block of stabling and outbuildings to one side at the back, she realised that this was the end of her short but happy relationship with Polly. This was Polly's home – where she lived for some of the year. Possibly she was stabled during the colder months of winter. Polly knew this house and driveway well – her head was held high, her ears pricked and she walked with an excited step.

As Jess kicked her feet out of the stirrups and slid down from the saddle, the misery which had remained dormant all morning suddenly came to the surface, taking her by surprise. Blinding tears leapt to Jess's eyes and chased each other down her cheeks. She flung her arms around Polly's neck and sobbed into the arab pony's dark mane. Polly stood very still, turning her beautiful head to nudge Jess's arm gently. Jess pulled a handkerchief from her anorak pocket, wiped her wet face and blew her nose. Polly snorted hopefully at the handkerchief and, despite her misery, Jess found herself laughing again.

"Trust you to think it's food!" she said, stroking Polly and smoothing the long strands of forelock which hung delicately about the brow-band. "Sorry about that, Polly," she continued. "I shouldn't be such a baby. I've brought you home to Beckie. You haven't seen Beckie for *ages* – and she's longing to see you. Come on!"

Allowing herself a large sniff and a further quick rub with the handkerchief, Jess resolutely led Polly towards the front door and rang the bell. Almost at once, the door was opened and there stood Mrs Stockwood, beaming with pleasure.

"Jess! You're here – how lovely! Would you like to take Polly round to the back. There's a ring outside the stable – you can tie her up there, if you will. Then I'll take you in to meet Beckie."

Jess led Polly round to the back of the house. As she replaced Polly's bridle with the head-collar, which she had secured to the pommel of the saddle before leaving Trumpeter Cottage, Jess found herself wondering how Beckie Stockwood was feeling. As she tied the rope to the ring in the wall, unfastened the girth and lifted the saddle from Polly's back, she wondered if she and Beckie would like each other as much as they had seemed to in their letters. Being reticent by nature, Jess tended to be wary of new relationships, and she felt nervous as she propped the saddle against the stable wall and hung the bridle from a convenient hook.

"There you are, girlie," said Jess, proffering the carrot which Polly knew had been lurking in Jess's pocket, "I expect Beckie will be out to see you shortly," she added, giving Polly a final hug before retracing her steps to the front door of Horwood House.

"Come in, dear," said Mrs Stockwood warmly. "Beckie's longing to meet you. I'll get you both something hot to drink – you must be cold after that ride on this chilly morning."

"Oh no, really – it's a lovely morning for riding."

"Well, I'll get you something anyway – and I'm sure you won't say no to one of my home-made cakes!" She led the way to a room at the front of the house. "Beckie's here, in the living room," she said. "You two get acquainted, while I fetch a tray." She opened the door. "Here we are, Beckie darling. Here's Jess."

It was a lovely room. The furnishings, of yellow and orange, seemed to echo the bright flames of the coal fire that burned brightly in the grate. Comfortable-looking chairs were drawn up to the fire and a small table stood to one side of where Beckie sat. Bright sunshine streamed in through the windows and the French door.

Mrs Stockwood left Jess, who stood awkwardly, just inside the door. It wasn't just that Jess felt suddenly shy at meeting this friend whom she had known only by correspondence. Jess was speechless as Beckie smiled up at her. For Beckie Stockwood was looking at her from a wheelchair.

Fourteen

"I should have told you," said Beckie, sipping at her coffee. She pushed the plate of cakes towards Jess. "Go on, have one. Mum will be disappointed if you don't. I think she's been looking forward to you coming over as much as I have! I was hoping to be out of this thing by now," Beckie explained, tapping the wheelchair with her hand, "but everything seems to take so long." She looked across the table at Jess. "I'm sorry I didn't say anything in my letters – did it surprise you to see me in a wheelchair?"

Jess suddenly felt very hungry. She chose a large slab of chocolate cake and bit into it. "Well . . . yes," she admitted. "I thought you must be feeling very weak with being in hospital for so long, and that was why you didn't come out to see Polly."

Beckie hesitated before she spoke. "I don't think I *will* come and see her – not . . . not this time. I want to wait until I can stand and walk properly – and *ride* her." She looked at Jess to see her reaction. "You must think I'm crazy! But I'd rather wait. I'll watch when you go—"

"But I thought – I thought – you wanted Polly . . ."

Beckie looked puzzled. Then, as she realised, her face was full of consternation. "Oh, Jess, I'm sorry. I didn't think. I didn't realise. You were bringing Polly back to me, weren't you – for good?"

Jess nodded. "Oh dear," Beckie sighed, "I don't seem to be getting anything right. I can't get walking yet. I want to *so* badly. And I want Polly back, too. But . . . but, I just want to get out of this thing. You understand, don't you?"

"Yes, I think I do," Jess replied slowly, remembering the feeling of cantering on Polly, the powerful body beneath her and the feeling that she was floating on air – flying almost. She could imagine how trapped Beckie felt, how she wanted to be free of the constraints of the chair before she even touched her beloved Polly again.

"I do, really I do," Jess repeated.

"So you don't mind taking Polly back and looking after her for a bit longer for me?"

Jess shook her head, laughing. "Of course not!"

Beckie's brown eyes were serious as she looked at Jess. "I think you feel the same about Polly as I do," she said, slowly, "and it must hurt to have to give her up after all these weeks. But I'll *share* her with you, Jess. And I'm sure you'll have your own pony one day – one just like Polly."

"Yes, one day . . ." Jess sighed and reached forward for another of Mrs Stockwood's delicious cakes.

So, there were still two ponies in the orchard at Trumpeter Cottage. Jess reminded herself, daily, that Polly would soon be gone for good.

"You see, Polly," Jess explained, from her usual seat on top of the orchard gate, "I'll be able to see you when I go to see Beckie. And, like Stan Croxford and Beckie said, I'll have my own pony one day – but it'll have to be just like you!"

"Can't I have a *little* ride on Muffin?" Tommy, sitting next to Jess, turned pleading eyes in her direction.

"Tom, you know what Mum said."

Tommy kicked at the gate. "But it's not fair," he wailed.

"Cheer up, Tommy," said Jess. "Mum and Dad will let you ride, I'm sure they will. One day, you'll ride and I'll have a pony that really is mine. We've just got to be patient." She jumped down from the gate. "Come on! Time to go – we're all off Christmas shopping this afternoon."

When Jess cycled over to Currington Bayley on the following morning, Beckie opened the front door from her wheelchair. Her eyes were shining.

"Doctor James is coming to see me on Monday," she told Jess excitedly. "I've been doing all my exercises – I'm sure he'll be pleased with me."

When Jess left, she arranged to visit Beckie later in the week, after the school term had finished.

It was just a week to Christmas. Life at Trumpeter Cottage was very busy. Christmas decorations were brought out from their boxes, and soon the cottage glittered and glowed with tinsel and paper chains. The Christmas tree, which had been chosen during the shopping trip, was carried into the lounge and decorated. Jess climbed one of the old apple trees in the orchard to retrieve some mistletoe from its topmost branches, and Dad cut armfuls of holly from the bush at the back of the orchard.

"Doesn't it look lovely!" Mum said on Sunday evening, when everyone had finished.

Jess looked round at it all – the decorations, the tree, Clare, Kim and Tommy propping up the Christmas cards, Badger flopped in front of the fire and the kittens chasing each other over the settee. She sighed with pleasure. Their first Christmas at Trumpeter Cottage was nearly here.

The school term finished on Wednesday morning. Jess changed from her school clothes into jeans and a sweater as soon as she arrived home.

"I'm going to see Beckie this afternoon," she informed her mother, "so can I get myself a quick lunch? Then I can be away from Beckie's home early and be home before dark. I'm taking her Christmas present."

"Yes, dear, of course – and why don't you ask Mrs Stockwood to bring Beckie over, now you're on holiday. I'm sure we could manage the wheelchair. The front door's quite wide, and those double doors into the lounge would easily give enough room."

"Great idea, Mum – I'll ask."

Jess hummed to herself as she cycled along the lanes to Currington Bayley. In the haversack on her back was Beckie's present – a large drawing block and a drawing pen.

At Horwood House, Jess propped her bicycle against the wall and rang the front door bell. Several minutes passed before the door was opened. It was Mrs Stockwood who stood in the doorway.

"Oh . . . Jess . . ." Mrs Stockwood's face looked drawn and tired. "I'm sorry, I didn't know you were coming. I'm afraid Beckie isn't well. I can't let you see her – I'm sorry, Jess."

Fifteen

Jess's return journey was much slower, as she puzzled over Beckie's sudden illness.

"What do you think is the matter, Mum?" she asked when she arrived home. "I didn't like to ask. Mrs Stockwood looked so worried."

"I'll ring her tomorrow," Mum promised. "Better not bother them today. Maybe it's a relapse. Beckie did have a very bad accident, you know."

Mum telephoned the next day and, after a long conversation with Mrs Stockwood, she returned to the kitchen looking thoughtful. "Don't worry," she told Jess, "Beckie's getting better . . . poor girl, she hasn't been very well. She's going to write to you as soon as she can."

"But Mum, she's all right, isn't she? What's the matter with her?"

"Let her tell you herself, Jessie," Mum replied, quietly.

The next few days leading up to Christmas were so full that Jess did not have much time to wonder about Beckie. There was more shopping, presents to wrap, mince pies to make and relatives to visit. Jess rode Polly and Muffin every day, and watched the post for a letter from Beckie, but nothing arrived.

Then, at last, it was Christmas Eve, with Tommy rushing excitedly around the lounge, Christmas carols, with Mum playing the piano, and everyone staying up later than usual.

Lying in bed at midnight, Jess listened to the church bells ringing. As she drifted off to sleep, she wondered how Beckie was feeling. But her last thought, as she fell asleep, was of Polly, quietly cropping the grass in the orchard, with Muffin.

"Wake up, Dess, wake up!"

It was Tommy, wide awake at half past five in the morning, tugging at Jess's sheet.

"Tommy, it's still night. I only just went to sleep."

"But it's Christmas, Dess. You haven't opened your stocking. Look what I had in mine!"

He blew screechingly down her ear through a toy trumpet – and Jess relinquished all hope of further sleep. She buried herself under her duvet and called out from her warm cave, "Tommy! I'll only get up if you stop that awful noise." The trumpet stopped.

"OK I give in," she said, emerging and sitting up in bed, yawning and groping for her Christmas stocking.

It was a family rule that no one opened the special presents around the Christmas tree until after breakfast.

"Come on – eat something sensible," Mum urged. "You can't all have a diet of chocolate Father Christmases!" But no one took much notice.

Dad had to be hauled from his Christmas lie-in, since it was another family rule that the whole family had to be there before presents were opened. Then began the handing over of presents, the frantic rustle and tear of paper and exclamations of delight.

Jess saved her present from Mum and Dad until last. There was a parcel and an envelope. Jess unwrapped the parcel.

"Oh, it's a lovely picture," she breathed, gazing at the beautiful, grey arab pony which looked out at her from the frame, its head thrown high and its mane lifting in the breeze. "It's just like Polly."

"That's what we thought," said Dad.

A squeal of delight came from the other side of the Christmas tree. Tommy was also opening his present from Mum and Dad. His round, pink, beaming face was topped by a small, black riding hat.

Jess looked towards her mother. "Does that mean—"

"Yes," Mum smiled. "I've given in. You can take Tommy out on Muffin. We're going to let him have some riding lessons, too."

Jess turned to her father. "But, Dad, is that all right . . . I mean . . . can you . . ."

"Yes, Jessie," Dad replied, anticipating her question. "Things are much better at work now. Mr Davies called me in last Monday. The firm has had a much better half-year – and I've been given that promotion at last!"

"Dad, that's wonderful!"

Jess turned her gaze to the picture of the grey arab. The more she looked at it, the more it looked like Polly, poised at the top of a hill, ready to canter down, her banner tail flowing behind her, her beautiful, fine head held proudly . . .

"Don't forget your other present," Mum said, pushing the envelope towards Jess.

Jess opened the envelope. Inside was a folded piece of paper. Opening it, Jess read:

> "If your present you want to find
> Out in the garden you must go.
> It's somewhere there if you just look
> So hurry up – don't be slow!"

"Whatever does this mean?" Jess asked, turning puzzled eyes towards her parents.

"Just what it says," said Dad, grinning at her. He caught hold of Tommy's hand. "Shall we go and help her, Tom?" he asked.

Kim and Clare gathered round, reading out the rhymed message. "What is it?" said Kim. "Some flowers, do you think?"

"A tree!" suggested Tommy.

"Or a lake!" stated the more ambitious Clare.

"Don't you know either?" asked Jess. The two girls shook their heads.

"Come on!" shrieked an excited Tommy, "a treasure hunt!"

The whole family, including Badger and the kittens, followed Jess into the garden. Badger thought that they were all quite crazy, and stood with puzzled eyes and gently waving tail, watching the four Caswell children wander up and down the garden, peering at the ground and up at the trees. The three kittens thought that this was a glorious new game and spent their time leaping out at the children and each other from behind the cabbages.

"I can't see anything," Jess admitted.

"Nor me," agreed Kim.

"I'm cold," said Clare.

A shrill whinny sounded from the direction of the orchard.

"It's Polly," said Jess. "She's heard us." She hurried in the direction of the orchard, but when she rounded the corner by the coal shed, she came to an abrupt standstill.

"What's Polly doing in the stable?" Jess exclaimed.

"And what's that flapping on her neck?" said Kim. Jess hurried over to the stable. Polly whinnied again – a soft, welcoming sound – as Jess approached. She pawed the ground impatiently.

Jess put her arm round the pony's neck. "You don't like being in here, do you, girlie? You're used to the orchard." Her hand touched something – a piece of card. "Whatever . . ." Around Polly's neck was a piece of string, and attached to the string was a large Christmas card. Looking inside, Jess read, "Happy Christmas, to Jess with love from Mum and Dad."

Jess felt herself go pale. It couldn't mean what it seemed to mean. It wasn't possible. She must be misunderstanding. She swung round. There were Mum and Dad, smiling at her.

"Happy Christmas, Jess," said Dad.

"But . . . but . . ."

"She's yours, Jessie," said Mum. "Polly's yours."

"But . . . she can't be. Polly belongs to Beckie . . ." Jess felt close to tears. She had just been told that she could have what she wanted more than anything else in the world, but it didn't seem possible. She wondered, briefly, whether she was having a tortured dream and soon she would wake. Polly nudged her shoulder. She felt real enough.

Mum stepped closer. "She really *is* yours now, Jess," she repeated, gently. "It was Beckie's idea.

100

She was determined about it, once she decided. She had some bad news, you see, last Monday – from Doctor James. That's why she wouldn't see you on Wednesday."

"But, what—"

"Doctor James told Beckie that she may never walk again. They kept hoping and hoping at the hospital, but . . . well, now they think that her back is too damaged."

"But, Mum, that's awful. I can't take Polly away from her – especially now."

Mrs Caswell put an arm around her daughter's shoulders. "Beckie was desperately upset when she was told," she explained. "She's coming over after lunch – and Mr and Mrs Stockwood. They're staying to tea. She didn't write a letter after all, because she wanted you to have a surprise."

As they walked slowly back to the cottage, Jess continued to question her mother. "How long have you known about this, Mum?" she asked.

"Only since Thursday, when I spoke to Mrs Stockwood on the phone. Beckie was absolutely determined about it, she said. They wouldn't take the proper amount for Polly, either. Beckie said that it *must* be you who had Polly – otherwise she couldn't bear to part with her."

For the rest of the morning, Jess divided her time between helping Mum with the vegetables, and gazing disbelievingly at Polly, who was back in the orchard with Muffin. Christmas lunch was a ritual which she hardly noticed. She *had* to see Beckie.

At four o'clock, the Stockwoods' car drove down the drive and came to a halt outside the front door. The two sets of parents greeted each other and Mr Stockwood took the wheelchair from the boot of the car. Then he lifted Beckie out and sat her in the chair. Beckie waved to Jess, who hung back.

"Happy Christmas, Jess!" She waved a parcel in Jess's direction. As Jess came up, she said, before Jess had a chance to speak, "Take me to see Polly, *please*, Jess." Then, thrusting the parcel into her hands, she added, "and I hope you like this."

"Thanks." Jess was glad to be able to grasp the wheelchair handle and escape the watching eyes of the parents. "You shouldn't have," she added.

"Of course I should, silly!" said Beckie, laughing. "Your present was super – just what I wanted. I'm going to draw a lot more from now on – that's one of the things I decided this week. I really love drawing, and I think I want to be an artist."

"Your drawings are really good," Jess told her, as she guided the chair carefully over the path leading to the stable. Beckie could use the chair herself, but the uneven ground made it hard work. Jess sat on the wall while she opened the parcel from Beckie.

"Beckie! How did you know?" Jess examined the grooming kit delightedly. "I've only got an old dandy brush that Rachel let me have when I looked after Beetle." She pulled out the contents. "Look! Even a comb – I'll be able to comb Polly's tail . . . Beckie!"

"Yes?"

"I can't take Polly from you."

"Why not?" demanded Beckie. "It seems sensible to me."

"Sensible?"

"Yes. Don't you see?" Beckie paused. Then she began again, talking quickly. "Now look. I love Polly. I want to ride her. But I can't. I just *can't*. It's no good beating about the bush. If I don't walk again, I shan't be able to ride her again – ever."

"But people do ride ponies," Jess put in, "disabled people, I mean."

"I know," Beckie replied. "I asked Doctor James about it. But he said that it would be a long time before I could – and even then I would have to go to a special centre, where they have helpers and very quiet ponies."

Beckie, who had been looking down as she spoke, looked up now. Despite the seriousness of her eyes, she smiled ruefully. "Neither of us can say that Polly is quiet and docile, can we? Much as we love her and know how gorgeous she is to ride, we both know that she's ... well, flighty, at times!" Grudgingly, Jess agreed.

"You know when you came on Wednesday," Beckie continued. Jess nodded. "Well, I had been crying for two days – since Doctor James came and told me. Then, when Mum told me that you'd been – well, I stopped at last! And then I started thinking. And then Doctor James came again." Beckie chuckled. "He said he had given me the normal two days for crying! He's really nice," she added, seriously. "We had a long talk, and that's when I realised that *you* must have Polly."

"But I still don't—"

"Jess, I *know* how you feel about Polly because I feel the same. I saw you, you see, when you brought Polly to me when I came back from hospital. I saw you have a good howl when you thought you were saying goodbye to Polly. Well, that's just what I did, too. And I really am saying goodbye to *riding* Polly. But I'm lucky because I shall be able to see her any time by coming to see you."

"Or I'll bring her to see you."

"That's right." Beckie paused. "And I was hoping that you and Polly would help me to live with this," she added, looking down at the wheelchair.

Jess was quiet for a moment. Then she said, slowly, "I'll go and fetch her, then, shall I?"

Beckie grinned. "Great!"

Collecting the head-collar from the shed, Jess made her way to the orchard, where Polly and Muffin waited, expectantly. They had heard the voices.

"I'll be there shortly with a feed," Jess promised Muffin as she slipped the head-collar on to Polly.

Jess opened the gate and the grey pony stepped daintily through the muddy opening, looking about her eagerly and snorting in the crisp December air.

"Polly!" Beckie called, and the grey arab whickered. "Oh, Jess, she's even lovelier when you haven't seen her for six months."

Polly pranced sideways, snorting noisily and eyeing the wheelchair with suspicion.

"You'll have to get used to it, Polly," Beckie told her. "It's going to be with us for a long time."

"Beckie."

Beckie turned to her friend. "Yes?"

"Let's share her. Let Polly be ours."

Beckie laughed. "Jess Caswell, when will I make you understand? OK," she added. "We'll say that Polly is ours. But I've had my turn – now it's yours."

Beckie smiled up at Jess, but her eyes were serious as she spoke again.

"She's yours now, Jess."

DREAM
PONY

Chapter 1

"But, Beckie, *why*? I mean . . . you can't . . . you can't . . . "

"I know . . . "

On the other end of the telephone, Beckie's voice sounded detached, Jess thought.

"I know," Beckie repeated. "I can't *ride* him. But it's made Mum and Dad happy," she added. "They try so hard . . . " There was a small silence. "He *is* rather sweet," Beckie concluded.

"I'd love to see him— "

"When can you come?" Beckie broke in, her voice brightening.

"I'll have to wait till the weekend."

Jess could almost feel the disappointment running down the telephone line to her from Beckie's end. "Sorry, Beckie," she added, hastily, "but there seems to be more homework this term."

There was another silence, and then Beckie spoke again. "Oh, I *wish* . . . "

"What?"

"Nothing."

Disappointment was heavy in Beckie's voice, so Jess said quickly, "Shall I come on Saturday, then?"

109

"Oh, yes! And you'll come on Polly, won't you?"

When Jessica Caswell had replaced the telephone receiver, she sat huddled on the floor beside the telephone table. She hugged her knees, which were pulled up under her chin. Miserably, she gazed into space. It wasn't going to work. She had never thought it would – not deep down inside her. Polly had been *Beckie*'s pony and Beckie loved her still, just as Jess did. Jess sighed.

"What you doing there, Dess?" Four-year-old Tommy's round, cheerful face appeared just above Jess's line of vision.

"Thinking," his elder sister replied, noncommittally, still gazing blankly ahead of her.

"What about?"

"Things."

Finding himself unable to extract any further information, Tommy trotted on his way through the hallway of the cottage, towards the kitchen, while Jess resumed her brooding.

Before her telephone conversation with Beckie, Jess had been out into the cold January night to feed her two ponies by moonlight. Muffin, the stocky little twelve-hand chestnut pony, belonged to the Carters, who lived in the next village. While Elizabeth Carter, their daughter, was abroad at college, Jess was looking after Muffin. Although he was too small for Jess, it had

110

been wonderful to have a pony to ride during the summer holidays. Any pony was better than none, Jess had wisely decided, and Muffin was cheerful and friendly, if a trifle lazy.

Then Polly had come into Jess's life. Polly, the beautiful grey arab mare, whom Jess had loved from afar. When Jess had been asked to look after Polly while her owner, Beckie Stockwood, had been in hospital, Jess's happiness had been almost complete. The only cloud on the horizon had been the knowledge that, one day, Polly would have to go back to her rightful owner.

Then, a terrible blow for Beckie had made a dream come true for Jess. When Beckie had been told by doctors that she might never walk again, she had insisted that Polly should belong to Jess, who loved her as Beckie did.

But it wasn't going to work, Jess repeated to herself, staring meditatively across the dim hallway where, only a few weeks ago, Christmas decorations had hung and carols had drifted in the air. It had been the Caswells' first Christmas at Trumpeter Cottage, and the best that Jess had ever known, with her own pony at last. Polly was so lovely; she was the pony of Jess's dreams, but—

"Jessie, what*ever* are you doing out here?" Mum's voice interrupted Jess's reverie. Jess sighed. This time she would not get away with the monosyllabic replies which she had given to Tommy's questions. Mum, sympathetic to her eldest daughter's introverted moods, would want to know – and to help.

"It's Beckie," Jess began, "she just telephoned. Her parents have bought her another pony!"

"But . . . " Mum looked puzzled. "Why does that make you look so miserable? Surely that's good news, isn't it?" Mrs Caswell paused and looked thoughtful. "Although I don't quite understand why they've bought her *another* pony, when she couldn't ride the one she had, poor girl."

"That's just it, Mum," Jess put in, hurriedly. "I think that's why they must have bought it – because Beckie's *pining* for Polly. She loves her, Mum, and she wants her back, I *know* she does." Jess slumped her chin down again onto her knees. "I know you and Dad gave me Polly as a present, and that you paid Beckie's parents for her, but I can't keep her if Beckie really wants her, can I?" Jess turned miserable eyes towards her mother. "Poor Beckie, Mum. It's bad enough having to spend the rest of her life in a wheelchair, without someone else taking the pony that she loves and that she wants as her own!"

Mother and daughter looked at each other for a moment, in silence. Then Mum spoke. "Jess, I'm sure you're imagining things. You know, you're much too serious and imaginative sometimes. Now look . . . " Mum rested a reassuring hand on Jess's shoulder. "Why don't you go on into the living room by the fire, with the others, and get on with that homework you were telling me about at teatime. I'll try to have a quiet word with Mrs Stockwood. Then, when you see Beckie at the weekend, you can ask her, properly."

It was comforting to take Mum's advice; to sit, cross-legged by the hearth in the warm room with Clare, Kim and Tommy, and with Dandy, Jess's young cat, curled up on her knee, a contented ginger ball of purr. It was even good to frown over the list of French verbs which had to be learned for tomorrow's test.

In front of the fire, eight-year-old Kim lay reading, and near the window Clare, a year older than Kim, rested one hand on the table edge, practising her ballet movements. Tommy crawled around the furniture, clicking his tongue in a somewhat bizarre attempt at imitating the sound of horses' hoofs as he played with his Christmas present from his three sisters. Jess had made wool-covered pipe-cleaner ponies of various colours, together with riders, and Clare had clothed the riders and cut out and sewn tiny felt saddles and bridles for the ponies. Kim had cut, glued and painted a row of cardboard stables, complete with mangers, and hinged doors with paper-clip bolts. The combined present had been a huge success and now, as January was coming to a close, Tommy seemed to have completely renounced his toy cars in favour of the home-made stables and ponies.

Yes, Jess thought, leaning against the warm stone of the hearth, it was better to be in here with the others than by herself, worrying. But, nevertheless, the worry niggled on, turning her dreams later that evening almost to nightmares. Polly, her beautiful, graceful Polly, tossing her small arab head, swishing her long fine mane this way and that, before cantering away, further and further, until she was lost from sight for ever . . .

this morning," she explained. "But," she added quickly, before Tommy had time to protest, "I'll take you for another half-hour tomorrow." She grinned at him, conspiratorially. "We'll stretch it out a bit, tomorrow," she said. Tommy looked puzzled. "I'll forget to look at my watch," Jess explained.

As realisation came, a beatific smile spread across Tommy's round, pink face. Giving Muffin a quick pat, he ran indoors to have his breakfast.

With Tommy's early morning ride successfully completed, Jess left Muffin in Tommy's charge while she gave Polly a quick groom. When entrusted to his four-year-old rider, Muffin was a model of decorum. He adored Tommy, and seemed to sense that he was very young.

Muffin stood patiently while Tommy groomed him yet again, and he walked quietly when Tommy led the chestnut pony back to the orchard.

" 'Bye, Tommy," Jess called from Polly's saddle. "Go and tell Mum we've finished the ride."

" 'Bye," Tommy echoed, trotting back obediently towards the cottage. Jess grinned to herself. She knew very well that Tommy would be back in a few minutes, and would probably stand by the gate talking to Muffin for the next half-hour at least. Tommy had become a truly dedicated pony person at a very young age!

But now, Jess forgot about Tommy while she enjoyed riding Polly. After nearly a week of not being ridden, Polly danced down the lane, her head high and her ears pricked so hard that the two pointed ends nearly touched in the middle. Polly snorted excitedly, and tossed her beautiful grey head, sending her long fine mane flowing about her neck and shimmering in the bright February sunlight.

Jess delighted in the lightness of Polly's step. She smoothed the pony's thickly coated neck and spoke to her softly. "You're excited, aren't you, girlie? You like being out," she crooned. "Well, next week, I think we'll be able to ride in the evenings. It's getting lighter every evening," Jess told her pony, "and I'll have time after school – for just a little ride, anyway. But won't it be lovely, Polly," she continued, ecstatically, "when the evenings are light and spring really comes? We can ride up to the common after tea. Won't it be wonderful, Polly?"

But Polly wasn't listening. She was too busy snorting at rustles in the hedge and prancing sideways past the grass verge, where the dry winter grass waved and crackled. For Polly, spring was here already, and it sent excitement thrilling through her.

Jess's thoughts turned to Beckie and Beckie's

new pony and her euphoric mood left her abruptly. Why had Beckie sounded so miserable on the telephone? She had sounded excited when Jess had said that she would be coming over to visit her, and had insisted that Polly should come, too. Was she really pining for Polly?

The thought of relinquishing Polly just when the beautiful pony of her dreams was really hers, filled Jess with horror. But if Beckie really did want Polly back, then she must have her – Jess was determined of that. Beckie had been through so much after the car accident, and to be left in a wheelchair was terrible. Jess knew she wouldn't be able to enjoy riding and loving Polly, if Beckie was secretly pining for her pony. She must ask her today. She *must* know . . .

Polly seemed to sense Jess's sombre mood, and the second part of their journey along Edgecombe Valley was more sedate. The gentle roar of the motorway droned to their right, as girl and pony trotted quietly along the lane towards Currington Brayley.

Horwood House was bathed in pale sunshine. Its weather-worn façade of mellowed brick glowed a gentle gold against the reddish-green of the ivy which clambered about its walls. Autumn leaves still gathered under the hedges, where snowdrops had pushed their way up towards the light.

Beckie was watching from the living-room

window, and before Jess and Polly had reached the front door she was there, smiling broadly as she moved her wheelchair deftly down the ramp which had been fitted over the steps. The Stockwoods were well off, and no expense had been spared in making life as easy as possible for Beckie, with her new mode of transport.

Beckie's brown eyes were shining as she reached up to stroke Polly's nose. The pony snorted and tossed her head.

"Silly girl! Isn't she beautiful?" Beckie asked, turning to her friend. Jess could only nod dumbly. It seemed that her fears were being justified already. Beckie had eyes only for Polly.

"It's great to see you, Jess," Beckie continued, excitedly, as she stroked Polly's neck with one hand whilst manoeuvring her wheelchair with the other. "Bring her round to the stables and then you can see Justin."

"Justin!" Despite her worries, Jess couldn't help grinning. It didn't sound like a pony's name, somehow.

Beckie laughed. "It does sort of suit him," she said, "He's really sweet."

From the way Beckie had talked of her new pony, Jess had expected something very small – perhaps even a shetland; a pony that Beckie could reach up to from her wheelchair. She was not prepared for the strong, muscular pony of about fourteen hands which stood in the stable behind Horwood House. The pony watched with interest as they all approached. While Jess and Polly stood back, Beckie unbolted the door.

"Stand still, Justin," she commanded, as she reached up with the lead-rope which she had been holding, and clipped it to the pony's head-collar. Justin stood quietly and even lowered his head for Beckie to fasten the buckles.

Moving her chair, Beckie led the pony out into the yard where he stood, turning his head inquisitively towards where Jess and Polly waited. To Jess, Justin seemed to be almost everything that Polly wasn't. He was black, with a small white star, and very strong, with short sturdy legs and a thick, muscular neck. Even so, he was a striking pony, with excellent conformation, a lovely small head, large, intelligent eyes and small, neat ears.

"He's nothing like I imagined," Jess admitted.

"He *is* sweet, though, isn't he?"

"He's *lovely*, Beckie. Really gorgeous," Jess agreed. As Jess looked at Justin, and watched Beckie moving him and talking to him, she realised that he was very well trained.

"What did you imagine he would look like?" Beckie asked, turning to look at Jess.

"Well . . . smaller, really," Jess admitted. "He's much bigger and stronger than I imagined." She hesitated. "It seems a pity . . . " She stopped then, wishing she hadn't begun this sentence.

"You think it's a pity I can't use him?" Beckie

said, cheerfully. She grinned at her friend. "But you haven't seen anything yet," she said, mysteriously.

Leading Justin back to the stable, Beckie tied him up outside. Then, moving her chair towards one of the sheds next to the stables, Beckie pulled back the bolt. Pushing back the door, she said, proudly, "There! What do you think of that?"

Pale February sunshine shone through the doorway. It illuminated yellow-painted woodwork and wheels, shiny black leather upholstery and two gracefully curving shafts.

"A trap!" Jess exclaimed. She looked at Beckie. "Then Justin, he's— "

"A ride and drive pony!" Beckie's eyes were shining again. "I've been out three times now," she explained. "It's really great!"

"But how do you manage?"

"Dad lifts me in. And Carol."

"Carol?"

"She's a student at Bristol. She lives quite close. Loves horses. It's a part-time job for her – to help eke out her grant. She comes in early in the morning to clean Justin out, exercise him and put out his hay." Beckie paused. "I bucket feed him," she added. "She comes again in the evening," Beckie continued, "and she can come twice a week at lunchtime too, for the afternoon. And on Wednesdays, she can come all day!"

"Your own groom!"

Beckie grinned. "Just about. Well, you know what a spoilt only child of rich parents, I am!" she added, laughing.

Jess turned to her quickly. "I know your parents are well off, but you're certainly not spoilt," she said, loyally.

"Well, I can have anything I want, can't I?"

"Except . . . "

"Yes, except to be able to walk." Beckie looked suddenly wistful. "And . . . "

Jess swallowed hard. She must ask Beckie — she must know . . . "And . . . Polly?" she asked, almost in a whisper.

Beckie turned round on her, open-mouthed. "Polly?" she said, incredulously. "Whatever would I want with Polly?" She laughed, ruefully. "Polly's beautiful. I love her. But I don't *want* her any more — not as my own pony. She's much too flighty. I want to draw her, though — that's why I specially wanted you to bring her today." Beckie looked towards Jess and spoke sadly. "No, it's not Polly I want." She sighed.

"Well, what is it, then?" Relief had returned Jess's voice to normal.

Beckie reached up and held her friend's arm. "Oh, Jess, I *wish* you could help me. Perhaps you can. It's Mum and Dad — I just can't persuade them."

"What, Beckie? What is it you want?"

"School!" Beckie replied, simply.

Chapter 3

"They won't let her, you see, Mum."

"Who won't, dear?" Mrs Caswell asked, vaguely, as she pricked the scrubbed potatoes with a fork and counted them at the same time. "Now, have I done enough?" she murmured. "Tommy seems to be eating more these days – it must be all this riding giving him an appetite."

"Only one hour a week!" Jess said, laughing. "But, Mum, I don't think you're listening," she added firmly. "Mr and Mrs Stockwood won't."

"Won't what?" Realising that her daughter's voice was worried, Mrs Caswell gave her all her attention.

"They won't let her go to school."

"But she *has* to go to school. It's the law."

"No, Mum, you *weren't* listening." Jess sighed as she opened the oven door of the old range, allowing Mrs Caswell to put the tray of potatoes in to cook. "Beckie has a tutor – a private tutor – who comes in every day to teach her. He's very nice and she likes the work, but . . . "

"She's lonely."

"Yes!" Jess looked at her mother with relief. Trust her to understand!

"Well, of course she is, poor girl," said Mum. "She must feel different enough, being in a wheelchair, without the added misery of being on her own, away from people of her own age."

"Well, why can't her parents see it – if *you* can?"

Mum stood up, looking thoughtful. "I expect they feel protective towards her now," she said, slowly. "Don't want her pushed around at school – and perhaps even bullied."

"Mm. You're right, Mum. That's what Beckie said." Jess sighed again. "They said they want her to have the best education because life will be difficult for her, being in a wheelchair. And, like you said, they're afraid she might get knocked around. But, Mum," Jess looked towards her mother, "school isn't like that. I'm sure people would be helpful."

"But, Jess, it will probably mean going away to a special school," Mrs Caswell said. "Had you or Beckie thought of that?" Jess shook her head. "Beckie might not like to be away," Mum added, "her parents may be right. But why don't you find out?" she concluded.

"Find out?" Jess looked taken aback.

"Go and see Mr Turner and ask him whether Beckie could come to school. It might not have any facilities for the disabled, you've got to think of that." Mrs Caswell looked at her daughter, questioningly. "Have you noticed any ramps at school, by the stairs – anything like that?" Jess

126

shook her head again. "Well, why not ask Mr Turner what he thinks," she finished. "Then, if *he* thinks Beckie could manage at school, you could try to persuade Beckie's parents."

"Well . . . I . . . "

"You want to help Beckie, don't you?" Mrs Caswell asked, gently. She knew what was running through Jess's mind. She would have to seek out Mr Turner, the headmaster, at school. She would have to speak up, come out of the shadows where she usually hid, anonymous and unnoticed. Jess the timid would have to become Jess the brave!

Jess hesitated outside the door. She raised one hand to knock, and then let it fall again. What shall I *say*? she thought desperately. Mr Turner, who boomed at them all in assembly, always looked so unapproachable. Tall and slightly stooping, he had a habit of taking off his glasses and staring intently at his gathered pupils, waiting until this device had quietened them all to silence before making his announcements.

Jess, who had been at Edgecombe Comprehensive for only one term, realised suddenly that she was in awe of Mr Turner – maybe even a little frightened of him.

Jess stared at the sign on the door. "C. Turner, Headmaster", stared back at her in plain black, no-nonsense lettering. She was wondering what the C stood for, when the sign disappeared and was replaced by the face of C. Turner himself, peering at her over the top of his glasses. Jess's stomach turned over a couple of times. As she began to stammer an explanation, Mr Turner broke in. "Ah, come on in," he said. "Mrs Brooks said you'd asked to see me. Jessica Caswell, isn't it?"

Stepping inside the room, and feeling like a prisoner being led into a courtroom, Jess heard the door close behind her. She sat obediently in the chair that Mr Turner pulled up for her.

"Now, then," said the headmaster, quietly. "What can I do for you, Jessica?"

It had been a very short ride but Polly had loved it. As she and Jess jogged back along Coalfield Lane, in that peculiar grey misty light which comes between late afternoon and evening, Jess felt content. The very fact that she and Polly had achieved a ride after school in the evening had put winter behind them, in Jess's mind. Probably, she reminded herself, there would be cold days to come, but now that the evenings were lengthening, all the pleasures of summer riding came nearer.

Just ahead, in the gloaming, the lights of a car approached, and then turned in through the gates of Trumpeter Cottage. That would be the Stockwoods, Jess thought, squeezing Polly into a trot. She wondered how Beckie would take her news.

Beckie was waiting in the dusk by the orchard gate. When Polly saw the shape of the chair and its occupant in the dim light, she jumped sideways, nearly unseating her rider. She stopped, snorting suspiciously, and throwing her head up high.

"It's only me, Polly," Beckie called, and the grey pony relaxed when she heard the familiar voice. She walked cautiously towards the wheelchair, pointing her nose in its direction and blowing loudly through her nostrils. A few yards from the gate, Jess halted and slid down from the saddle.

"You're a nutcase, Polly," she told the arab, smoothing her neck, reassuringly. "I sometimes wonder if you aren't too lively and excitable for me," she added, putting her arm around her pony's tense neck and hugging her to show her that she hadn't really meant it. There was a time though, much later, when Jess remembered her teasing remark with anguish . . .

"Well?" Beckie's voice was hopeful but tense. "How did you get on? What did he say?"

Jess pushed the stirrup iron up the leather and undid the girth. "It's difficult to say, really," she said, slowly, "whether I've got good news or not." She walked round Polly, pushed up the iron on the other side and swung the girth over, before lifting the saddle from Polly's back.

129

"Oh, Jess, *please* don't keep me in suspense," Beckie begged. "Can I go to your school or not?"

"Well . . . no. I'm afraid it's not on," Jess admitted, looking at her friend anxiously over the top of the saddle. She propped the saddle against the wall of the old shed and picked up the headcollar. "But don't give up hope," she added, quickly, "because I've got some better news for you, too."

"How do you mean?" Beckie asked.

Jess undid the throatlash, eased off Polly's bridle and slipped the headcollar over the pony's head. "Mr Turner says," Jess explained, leading Polly towards the stable where her bucket of food waited, "that it would be impossible for you to get about at our school. You wouldn't even get up to the front door because it's all steps."

"Oh— "

"But," Jess interrupted quickly, "he said that we're really lucky. We just happen to live in the right area. You *might* be able to go to Porterbury Comprehensive. That's the one just the other side of the motorway intersection. It's hardly any further for you than Edgecombe."

"But why— "

"There are only three in the whole country," Jess told her, excitedly, "and Porterbury's one of them!"

"But, Jess, what— "

"A comprehensive with a special unit for the

130

disabled!" Jess continued. "And ramps. *And* a special lift they had fitted last year, which goes up to the art department!" she finished, triumphantly.

"Jess! Really?" Now Beckie's voice was excited, too.

"But . . . " Jess spoke more quietly as she continued, "don't get too excited yet, Beckie," she warned. "Mr Turner is going to find out — he'll let me know tomorrow."

"What?"

"Whether there's *room* for you."

"Oh . . . I see." Beckie's voice, too, was subdued now.

"And even then, if there *is* room," Jess warned her, "there's still your parents."

"Yes."

"But Mum's probably working on them right now," Jess continued, cheerfully. "I told her all about it, and she's on your side. So— "

"It *might* happen!" Beckie finished off the sentence, and they grinned at each other. A grey nose pushed between them.

"Oh, Polly," Beckie breathed, her voice full of suppressed excitement. "Wish me luck!"

Chapter 4

By the end of the week, it was all settled. Beckie was to begin at Porterbury Comprehensive on the following Monday.

"What about Justin?" Jess asked her friend on Saturday morning. She had ridden Polly over to Horwood House, to find Beckie just returned from a drive. A tall girl of about nineteen, with short fair hair and a cheerful smile, had been introduced to Jess as Carol. Carol had lifted Beckie from the trap to her wheelchair, and now the two girls were sitting in the Stockwoods' front living room, while Carol unharnessed Beckie's pony and settled him in his stable with his hay. Polly, in the next stable, had also been given a drink and some hay.

"It's all going to work out quite well," Beckie told Jess. "Wednesday afternoon is sport, so I can be home by one o'clock on that day – Carol will pick me up in the car. And I can have almost half a day on Fridays, too, and on Mondays I can be home by three o'clock.

"Lucky thing!" said Jess, enviously. "I wish I could have time off to go riding!"

"Well, the idea is that it's good for me,"

Beckie explained. "Part of my treatment."

"You're still going to see Dr James at the hospital, aren't you?" Jess asked.

Beckie shrugged, dismissively. "Well, yes," she said, "I *do* go. And I do the exercises he's given me. But . . . "

"Beckie, you must keep going. If Dr James thinks— "

"He's very nice," Beckie admitted, "but . . . " she looked down, fiddling with the hard metal arms of her confining wheelchair as she spoke, "I think . . . " Beckie turned swiftly to look at her friend with serious brown eyes, "I think I . . . realise that . . . that I shan't walk again, Jess!" she finished, quickly. For a moment Beckie looked at Jess, her eyes dark with misery. Then she turned away quickly as Carol came in. Beckie busied herself with pouring out coffee.

As she talked and laughed with the other two, inside her head Jess was thinking, If only I could *help*. I'd even give up Polly if it would mean that Beckie could walk again.

After such a cheerful start, February became its true self. Grey, dismal skies emptied rain onto the countryside for day after day. The ground squelched underfoot, and Jess's two ponies stood forlornly in their three-sided shed, watching the rain lashing down. When they tired of this pastime, they grazed in the orchard, their backs

133

turned towards the south-west, their tails blowing in wet strands and their coats turned dark by the rain.

When Jess fed her ponies in the evenings, she put a bucket of food at each end of the shed, and hung up two nets of hay. She tried to rub dry the ponies' saturated coats, but it seemed to be an impossible task.

"It's hopeless," Jess complained to her father, one evening. "You don't think Polly ought to have a New Zealand rug, do you? Her coat isn't as thick as Muffin's."

"What does the expert say?" Dad asked, wiping his hands on the kitchen towel, having just finished the washing up with Jess's help. The expert was Miss Claremont, Jess's form mistress at school. Miss Claremont had owned her own pony when she had been at school and was still a pony lover. In fact, she had confided to Jess that she was considering owning a pony again.

"How did you know I'd asked Miss Claremont?" Jess demanded, looking surprised.

Dad crouched down in front of the stove. He pushed a poker between the bars, rattling it backwards and forwards to encourage the used coke and ashes towards the ash-pan. The old range at Trumpeter Cottage, named Old Grumpy by Mum, needed careful and constant attention. Dad straightened up and grinned at his eldest daughter. "I just had a feeling you

134

might have," he said. "And so what did she say?"

"That both the ponies are probably all right with their shed and their winter coats," Jess admitted. "She said that rugs are sometimes more trouble than they're worth. The ponies might get itchy and uncomfortable and might even get lice underneath the rugs, if I'm not careful." Jess frowned. "But it seems so awful, sometimes, to leave them out in the cold, while we're inside in the warm." Jess warmed her hands in front of Old Grumpy, who now glowed red between the metal bars.

"I expect Miss Claremont's right," Dad said, cheerfully. "The ponies are in their natural environment and you feed them well." He grinned at her again. "All those powders and potions you add to their food must keep them healthy. And their coats do grow especially dense for the winter weather," he added, hanging the poker back in its place beside Old Grumpy. "Polly's coat is quite thick, you know," he said. "It just happens that Muffin's is thicker."

When Jess went out to see the ponies again, later that evening, the rain had stopped. They were grazing at the far side of the orchard. Hearing Jess's call, Polly threw up her head, turning towards the sound. With a whicker of greeting, she set off across the grass at a trot, her dark grey banner tail floating out behind her.

135

Every turn and movement she made was a delight to Jess's eyes. "Polly, beautiful Polly," Jess murmured. She had let herself in at the gate, and now she put her arms around the pony's neck, as the grey mare turned her head to snort into the cold air. Soon came little Muffin, jogging across the wet grass, his thick thatch of mane bouncing on either side of his neck. A little chestnut nose pushed hopefully into Jess's hand.

Both ponies seemed cheerful and warm, Jess was relieved to see. She gave a handful of nuts to each, and then returned to the cottage.

Jess turned back as she reached the cottage door. Polly, silhouetted darkly against the night sky, still watched from the orchard. Jess's heart filled with joy. Life was almost too good, she thought superstitiously. A year ago, Jess had had no hope of ever having her own pony, and now she owned the most beautiful and gorgeous pony in the world! How could she be so lucky? Jess wondered, as she closed the cottage door, shutting out the night.

Chapter 5

The March winds came early, rushing through the February world and blowing away the signs of winter. Leaves swirled and twirled across the lawn at Trumpeter Cottage, hiding under the hedges before they were whisked away again and whooshed out into the lane. The three kittens, Dandy, Tabitha and Tibby, now eleven-month-old teenagers, chased the leaves and rushed up the apple trees in the orchard, their eyes dark with delight, and their tails twice their normal size. When Jess rode Polly in the twilight evenings, the pony danced and cavorted with the leaves, excited by the mischievous wind.

Beckie and Jess met only at the weekends during termtime. Beckie's telephone calls during the week were happy now. She was full of enthusiasm about life at Porterbury Comprehensive. "The art department is great," she told Jess. "I spend as much time there as I'm allowed!"

On the Monday of half-term, Beckie had an appointment at the hospital and Jess decided to take Polly up on to the common. The day was fine. A brisk wind sent thin white clouds scudding across the sky, and Polly danced down the lane from Trumpeter Cottage. Tommy, accompanied by Badger, the family dog, watched their departure from the garden wall.

"I'll take you for a ride later, Tom – promise!" Jess called, before she and Polly were blown round the corner and out of sight.

Jess let Polly jog along the lane. It had been a busy week at school, with plenty of pre-half-term homework, and there had been very little time for riding, so Polly was full of bounce.

"Spooky creature!" Jess told her, as Polly jumped sideways at the sight of a blackbird scrabbling in the dead leaves at the edge of the lane. But she laughed, nonetheless, and squeezed Polly on to a trot. It was a wonderful day for riding, and the half-term week stretched ahead, full of days with Polly.

Soon, pony and rider turned off the lane and up a rocky track. Polly knew where they were going, and she pulled strongly up the stony path towards the common. Still very steep, the path began to widen as the surface changed to the short, wiry grass of the common. Jess leaned forward, and Polly scrambled up the last few yards. At last, they were on the top.

Jess gazed about her, as Polly rested and blew breath. The view from the top of the common never failed to excite Jess. Below her, to the right, lay the wide green Edgecombe valley. On the other side of the valley, on a

high embankment, ran the motorway, with its continuous stream of toy cars. Jess turned her head and there was the sea to her left, glistening restlessly below. A sand-dredger chugged its way purposefully down-channel, leaving a V-shaped wake, and close to shore two sailing dinghies were sailing with the wind.

Turning round in the saddle, Jess saw Edgecombe Woods and the smooth slopes of the golf club.

"Right then, Polly," she said, turning back and looking towards the inviting paths which criss-crossed the common. "Let's have a good canter!" Polly needed no urging now that she had got her breath back from the climb. With a small buck, she was away. The paths on the common were narrow, widening in places. There were bushes to avoid, and in some places other riders had made jumps. Jess and Polly had just negotiated one of these obstacles – a couple of branches across the path forming a low brush jump – when they came face to face with a bay pony.

The pony was riderless. Reins flapped, and the pony threw up its head as it skidded to a halt. Polly, too, came to a halt. Jess acted quickly. She grabbed the pony's loose reins and squeezed Polly with her heels. Before they had time to argue, the two ponies found themselves walking together along the narrow path in the direction from which the bay pony had come.

Nice pony, Jess thought, eyeing Polly's bay companion. He was about Polly's size, but sturdier, a bright bay, with black points. His thick black mane bounced attractively about a strong muscular neck. Funny, Jess thought, he doesn't look the flighty type—

"Great! Thanks!"

A disembodied voice came from Jess's right. She halted the ponies as the bushes parted and a girl pushed her way through.

"Hi!" said the girl, grinning at Jess from a mud-splattered face. "Dr Livingstone, I presume!"

Jess giggled. "Is this your wild animal?" she asked.

The girl took hold of the reins and spoke firmly to the bay pony. "What got into you, pig? You know you *never* run off. And look what you did to me!" She stood back to show her pony the mud-covered state of her jodhpurs and anorak. Unimpressed, the bay pony nudged at her arm. The girl laughed and patted him affectionately, before checking the girth and remounting.

"It wasn't his fault," she admitted to Jess, as she settled herself into the saddle.

"What happened?" Jess asked. They walked their ponies on along the path, which had widened at this point.

"We were over there." The girl waved an arm vaguely to her right. "I saw this jump, you see. The ground was very muddy, and I suppose I sent him at it too fast." She wrinkled her nose. "And of course he slipped. He didn't fall, but he decided, at the last minute, that he didn't want to jump." She grinned across at Jess as she added, "But he didn't tell me in time, and I *did* jump! And *then*," she said, leaning forward to stroke her pony's neck, "while I was still sitting in the mud, something flew up right by him – a pheasant, I think – and he took off. He's not usually like that," she added, "it must be the weather!"

"Mine's spooky today, too," Jess agreed, warming to this cheerful girl. They walked their ponies on across the common, and Jess learned that her companion was about her own age, and that her name was Samantha Wilkes.

"But I'm Sam," she explained. "I'm only called Samantha at school, by the teachers." She leaned forward to pat the bay pony. "And this is Brecon," she told Jess. She pointed across the channel, to their left. "He came from the Brecon Beacons, over there in Wales, you see."

By the time they had reached the far end of the common, talking all the way, Jess and Sam were firm friends. Jess discovered that Sam went to Porterbury Comprehensive. When Jess told her about Beckie, Sam realised that she had noticed Beckie a couple of times, but had not actually met her.

"The only times I've seen her, she was on her way to the art department in the new lift," Sam explained. "I'll grab her next time and tell her I know you!"

Suddenly remembering Tom's promised ride, Jess parted from her new friend when they reached the gate into Winton Woods. They arranged to meet again the next day, to ride and to discuss further the topic which had occupied them for the last five minutes of their ride.

Jess had a lot to think about as she and Polly cantered back across the common towards home.

Chapter 6

"Jess, that's a great idea!"

"You'd be able to come, too, wouldn't you?"

"You try and stop me!" Over the telephone, Beckie's voice was excited. "I've got Justin – and the trap. And if we *do* decide to go ahead, I can do the organising – you know, the paperwork, letters and things. After all, I've *got* to sit here, so I might as well be doing things."

"I'll bring Sam in to see you tomorrow then, shall I?"

"Great!"

So, the next day brought Jess and Sam, riding into Lower Edgecombe on their ponies. Turning left at the crossroads, they followed the lane past the church and then on to Horwood House, where Beckie was waiting, impatient to meet Jess's new friend and to hear their news.

In the living room of Beckie's home, the introductions over, Beckie questioned Sam. "What did your friends say? Do they like the idea?"

"You bet!" Sam replied, "And . . . " She hesitated, before continuing, "My little brother's keen, too, but I told him he would be too young. He's only six."

Jess grinned. "My little brother's the same — but he's only four! I think, though," she added, more seriously, "we ought to have a lower limit of about eight, don't you?" The others nodded their agreement.

"We're decided then, are we?" Beckie had a notepad on her knee, over which a pen was poised. She looked at Sam. "I explained to Jess," she told her, "that if you're all agreeable, I can do the paperwork — be the secretary, I suppose."

"Good idea," Sam agreed. "So this can be our first meeting."

"What shall we call it?" Jess asked.

After a pause, Beckie said, "How about Edgecombe Valley? We all live in or near the valley."

"Yes, that sounds good," Jess agreed, "don't you think so, Sam?"

"Great!"

Mrs Stockwood came in with a tray, which she set on the table next to Beckie. Beckie handed round mugs of coffee. "We'll drink a toast, then," she said, excitedly, "to Edgecombe Valley Riding Club!"

Eight of them met on the following Thursday of half-term. Rachel arrived just before eleven o'clock, with her friend. They had ridden from the other end of the valley, beyond Porterbury.

"Poor old Bee doesn't know what's hit him,"

145

Rachel said, as she slid down from the saddle and stood outside the gate of Trumpeter Cottage. "He hasn't been for such a long ride for ages." She grinned. "And he doesn't realise that he has to go back, too!" Rachel Fielding lived nearly five miles away.

"Come on in," Jess said, opening the gate. "You can put Beetle in the orchard, if you like – he'll probably remember it." Jess reached up warily to stroke Beetle's dark brown neck, and received the expected nip.

"Ouch! Beetle, I can see you haven't changed your ways," she told him, rubbing her arm.

"Just one of your little idiosyncrasies, isn't it, Bee, old thing?" Twelve-year-old Rachel put an affectionate arm around her pony's neck, wincing when he repeated the treatment with her.

"Never mind, Beetle, I love you really," Jess said, laughing, but keeping a safe distance from Beetle's active teeth. It was nearly a year since Jess had taken Beetle as her first pony on temporary loan. Beetle was difficult and moody at times, but Jess had been thrilled to have a pony in the orchard at Trumpeter Cottage, to ride and to look after. By the time Beetle had returned to his rightful owner, little Muffin had been in residence.

"I'll just tie him up," Rachel said, leading Beetle along the path. "That's Dawn," she told

Jess, indicating her friend, "and the skewbald's Angus."

"Hi!" Jess called in the direction of the friend, who hadn't spoken.

The girl looked anxiously in Jess's direction and smiled uncertainly. When they reached the stable, Rachel tied up Beetle outside. Dawn looked about her, doubtfully.

"Here you are, Dawn. You can tie Angus up here." Jess said. She smiled at the girl, sympathising with her feelings of shyness. Jess, herself, had been a loner, feeling shy and uncertain of other people. But since meeting Beckie and caring for Polly, Jess had found it easier to mix. And after bearding Mr Turner in his den at school, nothing seemed impossible!

"Angus is a lovely pony," Jess ventured, looking in the direction of the sturdy skewbald pony. He was about fourteen hands, with strong shoulders and quarters, with a largish but attractive head, and big, intelligent eyes. "He looks a dear."

The other girl relaxed visibly. "Oh, he *is*," she agreed, with enthusiasm. She put an arm around the skewbald's neck. "I love him," she confided. She looked across at the stable, from where Polly was watching the proceedings with obvious interest. "Is that your pony?" Dawn asked.

Jess nodded. "Yes, that's Polly."

"She's beautiful," Dawn said.

"And quite naughty at times!" Jess laughed.

The others all arrived at once. As Beckie manoeuvred Justin and the trap carefully in through the open double gates of Trumpeter Cottage, much clattering of ponies' hoofs could be heard from down the lane.

Mrs Caswell came out to help Beckie. Jess lifted the wheelchair from the trap and opened it out, while her mother put one arm round Beckie. Justin stood quietly.

"Put your arms round my neck, Beckie," Mrs Caswell instructed, giving the girl a quick smile before slipping the other arm under Beckie's knees. "There you are! Out in a jiffy!"

"Thanks!" Beckie looked up at Jess's mother from her wheelchair, her eyes grateful for Mrs Caswell's businesslike approach.

The garden of the cottage was filling with ponies. As Jess led Justin over towards the vegetable garden, where she tied him up by the shed, three more ponies walked down the path, eyes bright with interest at the new meeting place and the sight of other ponies. Whinnies were exchanged, and one or two squeals.

Sam, leading the way, called out, "Hi, every-one!" She halted Brecon and turned round in the saddle. "That's Anna," she called, waving an arm towards the girl immediately behind her. The girl was tall, with long, straight fair hair and a serious face. She looked a little older than Sam. She rode a cobbish grey pony who viewed the meeting calmly from wide-set eyes beneath a straggly forelock.

"And behind her somewhere is Jackie," Sam added vaguely. Obviously feeling that this was enough introduction, she slid down from Brecon's saddle and led her pony over towards the stable, where Beckie greeted her from her wheelchair.

Jackie, obviously the youngest of the riders, hung back. She had a round, plump face, with dark hair curling from under her riding hat. Her pony, a stocky liver-chestnut, snorted suspiciously. Jackie jumped down and held his bridle tightly. "He gets a bit excited," she said to no one in particular.

Jess came forward. "Why don't you tie him over there, Jackie? Over by Dawn and Angus."

Last to arrive was a boy of about thirteen, astride a big scruffy bay cob. The cob pounded down the path and reined to an abrupt halt. The boy looked cheerful, with a freckled face and an untidy thatch of brown hair. He wore old-fashioned corduroy breeches, wellington boots and a roll-necked sweater. He announced himself as "Richard, from over the valley", and seemed to have heard about the club at school.

With all the ponies tied up, the eight gathered around Beckie's wheelchair, by the stable. Curiosity had brought Kim from Trumpeter Cottage, accompanied by Badger, who waved his tail amiably. Tommy, too, hovered on the edge of the gathering.

Jess cleared her throat. "Hello, everyone," she began, a little self-consciously. "We're having this meeting today as a sort of . . . trial." She looked round at them. "If we all enjoy it and think it's a good idea, Beckie, Sam and I will have another meeting and sort out the nitty-gritty – you know, membership fees and age limits, that sort of thing. And how often we want to meet. And, of course the sort of things we want to do. Is that OK?" Everyone nodded their approval.

"What is it, today?" Rachel asked. "You were a bit mysterious on the phone."

"I didn't know myself," Jess admitted. "Beckie's organised it. It's going to be a treasure hunt!"

Chapter 7

Before they split up into teams to go out on the treasure hunt, Rachel had confided to Jess, "I don't want to pair with Dawn, if possible. She's a bit of a drag, sometimes. That's why I was so pleased when you suggested this club. She's the only one I know near me who rides." Rachel sighed. "She's a bit wet." she said, dismissively.

"She's timid," Jess said, "I can see that. Perhaps riding with other people will help her. I know." She looked towards Copper, the little liver-chestnut pony. "How about Jackie? She seems a bit nervous, too. I'll put them together. You can go with Sam."

The small party of entrants was organised into two pairs and one threesome. Jess handed out pencils and paper, leaving the explanations to Beckie.

"The things you have to find are only small," Beckie said, "so you can put them in your pockets. Then you've got some clues to finding other things. When you find *those*, you have to write something on your piece of paper."

"Something?" Rachel echoed.

"Well, I can't tell you *what*, can I?" Beckie replied with a sigh. "It'll be obvious, if you guess the clue. And, Jess," Beckie added quickly, turning to her friend, "Your team will have to have a handicap, I'm afraid, because you might know a couple of the things I've given clues to." Beckie pulled out a large envelope from the side of her wheelchair. "Here you are, Tommy," she said, turning to him, "You can hand one of these sheets to every competitor." Tommy took the sheets, delighted to be taking part, even if only as a helper. "And then you can all begin," Beckie concluded, adding with a grin, "and may the best team win. We have some fantastic prizes, donated by grateful mothers, glad to be rid of their horsey offspring for the day!"

By one o'clock, it had begun to rain, but no one's spirits were dampened. It was only a slight drizzle, and it had been agreed that the hunt would be officially over by one fifteen, in order to give everyone time for their sandwiches, before the ride home.

The surprise of the day was that Dawn and Jackie were the winners. They arrived back at Trumpeter Cottage, damp but triumphant, with all the required objects and answers to Beckie's clues. Sam and Rachel, although already ensconced in the shed next to the stable unwrapping their packets of sandwiches, had given up on the last clue.

"But that was *easy*," said Beckie.

152

"It was gobbledygook as far as I was concerned," Sam admitted.

"And I was starving," Rachel added.

Beckie pulled out one of the sheets of paper. "'In the reign of Queen Victoria'," she quoted primly, reading from the paper, "'what time was it in Coalfield Lane in the afternoon?'"

Rachel mumbled something incomprehensible through her cheese sandwich, and Sam leaned forward. "What on earth was it, then?" she demanded.

"Half past four!" Beckie told them, triumphantly.

The two looked at each other and shrugged. "The girl's mad," Rachel concluded.

"Half past four?" Sam looked completely mystified.

"The post box, idiots!" Jess, Anna and Richard had just returned, and it was Jess who spoke from the doorway. "It's got Queen Victoria's name on it. You can see it's old." She sat down next to Rachel on a bale of straw, wriggling over to make room for Anna, who had followed her in. "And the afternoon pick-up time is half past four. *That* was easy," she added. "But it took me ages to think who Jeremiah Jockhill's bed-companion was!" She grinned at Beckie. "You've got a weird sense of humour," she told her. "It was Anna who suggested the churchyard."

"Dawn found them all!" Ten-year-old Jackie

153

Spalton spoke up from the corner of the shed, where she sat on a bale of hay.

Rachel looked across the shed at Dawn. "You must be brighter than I thought," she admitted, grudgingly. Dawn flushed with pleasure at this somewhat back-handed compliment.

For the next half-hour, a contented buzz of chatter filled the small shed. Outside, the drizzle had stopped and the ponies waited patiently.

At two o'clock, Jess called them to order.

"We thought we could have the meeting now," she explained. "About membership – that sort of thing." She looked round at them. "Do we all like the idea of the club?" Everyone agreed enthusiastically and soon the Edgecombe Valley Riding Club was officially inaugurated. It was decided that meetings would be held about once a month in term-time and once every fortnight in the holidays.

"I've typed out some membership forms," Beckie said, digging again into her large brown envelope. She handed them to Jess, who passed them round.

"How much will it cost to join?" Jackie asked. This prompted another discussion, at the end of which a figure of two pounds was decided, for the year. This, Beckie thought, should cover postage and paper and any unforeseen extras.

"What about people without ponies?" Dawn asked, timidly. "I've got a friend— "

"But we want to be a *proper* riding club, don't we?" Rachel broke in.

Anna, who had been quiet for much of the discussion, spoke up now. "*I* think we *should* let them join," she said, quietly. "I can remember what it was like not having a pony. I'd have loved to have joined a club like this . . . " She looked around at the others. "Just to see ponies and be near them . . . "

As Anna faltered and came to an embarrassed stop, Jess warmed to her, remembering her own non-pony days when she had longed so desperately for one.

"Of course! Anna's right," she exclaimed. "And more members will make it more fun. Don't you all think so?" she added, addressing the meeting.

There was a general murmur of assent. Rachel shrugged her shoulders, and Jess handed an extra form to Jackie. Sam leaned across and took another one as well. "There's this boy at school," she explained. "He hasn't got a pony, but sometimes he can borrow one."

When the others had gone, clattering noisily down the lane, Beckie wheeled herself in through the wide front doorway of Trumpeter Cottage. She and Jess settled themselves in the lounge.

"It went well, didn't it?" Jess said from her seat on the stone edging of the hearth.

156

"It was great," Beckie agreed. She frowned slightly. "I'm not sure about Rachel . . . "

Jess looked up quickly from stroking Badger, who was stretched in front of the fire, luxuriating in the warmth on a chilly February afternoon.

"Rachel?" Jess sounded surprised. "She's OK. She's just a bit . . . " Jess stopped to search for the right word before finishing, *"blunt!* That's what Rachel is. She rubs people up the wrong way sometimes. Got a heart of gold, though," Jess concluded with a laugh. Jess looked at Beckie across Badger's recumbent body. "You think she was a bit unkind to Dawn?" Beckie nodded. "She doesn't mean to be, I'm sure," Jess continued, fiddling with Badger's long black and white hair, twisting it between her fingers. "She just finds it difficult to understand people who aren't like her." She looked up again and grinned wryly at Beckie. "I know she thought I was wet when I met her first. I found it difficult to – to talk to people, and I was new at school." Jess laughed. "But by the time I'd had to deal with Beetle, I had plenty to say on *that* subject! And then we became friends."

Badger had given up hope of a quiet snooze. Instead, he settled for a tickle on his tummy, rolling over onto his back and grinning up at Jess. "Idiot dog!" Jess commented, obliging by tickling his fat stomach. "I think," she said to

157

Beckie, looking over at her friend with a grin, "that this club is going to be great. I'm really looking forward to the next meeting!"

But Jess didn't manage the next meeting, or the one after that. And neither did Polly.

Chapter 8

There was no warning. It seemed like any other day, that Saturday of the next meeting of Edgecombe Valley Riding Club. In fact, Jess thought, as she sat up in bed and looked out of her window at the clear sky slowly filling with early morning light, it was surely going to be a better day than usual. It was the weekend, it was a club meeting day, and it was almost the end of term. Only another few days at school, and then the Easter holidays! Wonderful, Jess thought as she padded barefoot along to the bathroom, humming quietly to herself.

Tommy was up before her, Jess noticed. His pyjamas were in a small heap on the bathroom floor, and the tiles around the washbasin were awash with water which Tommy had obviously aimed at his face but which had missed! Pushing the bathmat over with one foot and letting it soak up the water, Jess grinned to herself. Tommy wasn't the tidiest of people, but he was only four, after all.

Jess's own face-washing was purely academic, but at least the water reached its target. In two minutes flat, she was back in her bedroom, pulling on jodhpurs and a warm sweater and giving her dark hair a hasty brush. She had had it cut recently and now it was much easier to deal with. A quick brush in the mornings, and Jess could get on with the important things in life – going to see the ponies, and grooming and feeding them.

From her bedroom window, Jess could see the orchard where the ponies were kept and where Mum's hens wandered during the day. There were the hens now, spreading out across the orchard, strutting and clucking importantly. Mum or Tommy must have let them out. Nobody else would be up this early. It must have been Tommy, Jess decided a moment later, for there he was, running across the orchard, his little red wellies shining with dew. He seemed to be in a hurry, Jess noticed. He was probably rushing to find Mum, to ask if he could collect the eggs from the henhouse.

Tommy scrambled over the orchard gate, nearly falling before he reached the ground on the other side. Then, head bent, he ran towards the kitchen door. Jess smiled to herself as she turned away from the window, turning back again just for a moment to watch as Muffin came into view. Fat little Muffin, making his way quietly across the morning-wet grass, cropping slowly and methodically, his tail swishing gently. It must be habit, Jess reflected, for there

160

weren't any flies about yet. It was too early in the year.

As Jess opened her bedroom door, she thought she heard her name being called. As she stooped at the top of the stairs to pick up Dandy, who had come up to find her, she definitely heard it.

"Dess! Dess!" It was Tommy's high-pitched little voice. Jess held Dandy close to her, feeling the young cat's body reverberating with purrs. She hurried down the stairs, two at a time. Tommy's voice had sounded strangely urgent. Perhaps there was something wrong. Maybe a fox had got into the henhouse.

Jess reached the bottom of the stairs as Tommy entered the hall. He was still wearing his boots, despite a family rule that boots should be left in the passage outside the back door. Seeing the trail of muddy bootmarks across the kitchen floor, Jess was about to open her mouth in protest, but Tommy's words came first, freezing her own words so that they were never said.

"Dess!" Tommy panted. "Polly's ill!" He was so out of breath that he could hardly get the words out.

"What?" A chill spread through Jess's body. "What's wrong? Tell me, Tommy. Quickly!"

Tommy's eyes were big and troubled. "She – she looks – *funny*," he said. But he wasn't laughing. For a four-year-old, Tommy was very serious-minded, and whatever he wanted to communicate to his sister, it was obviously something serious. Dropping Dandy to the floor and pushing past Tommy, Jess raced for the kitchen door. She pushed her feet into her wellingtons and was out across the garden towards the orchard as if she were being chased by a thousand demons. She didn't think, she just ran. Leaping the gate, she raced across the grass until she came within sight of Polly.

Jess halted. For a moment, relief flooded over her. Polly was all right. Surely she was? She was just standing in the middle of the orchard. There was no sign of a broken leg, or some terrible bleeding gash; she wasn't rolling on the ground in agony. All these things had raced through Jess's mind when Tommy had told her that Polly had looked "funny". Slowly, Jess began walking towards her pony. "Polly," she called, softly, waiting for her to turn her head and whicker a greeting. But Polly did nothing. She just stood, firmly and squarely in the orchard. She seemed to be staring into space. Jess's relief quickly vanished and the fear returned.

She ran to the pony's side. "Polly, Polly! What is it? What's the matter?" Jess stroked the familiar grey neck. The muscles were tight beneath her hand and Polly was sweating slightly. What was it? Some kind of fever? Jess spoke to her pony again, waiting for one ear to flick back to listen and the beautiful head to turn in recognition. But there was no response. Polly's ears remained forward, and she continued to look straight ahead. Jess bent down and pulled some grass, offering it to Polly on her hand. Slowly, carefully, the pony took the grass and tried to eat, but after a moment the grass just fell to the ground.

"What's wrong with her, Dess?" Tommy had arrived at Jess's side, and he whispered the words, almost as if he were afraid of waking Polly.

"I don't know, Tommy." Jess, too, was almost whispering. She turned to her small brother. "But we must get help – quickly." She put a hand on his shoulder. "Can you go indoors and find someone – Mum – anyone. Ask them to telephone the vet, and ask him to come as quickly as possible." Jess turned back to her motionless pony and her voice broke as she said, "It's something serious – I'm sure of that." By the time she had turned back to Tommy, he had gone, across the orchard and over the gate to the house.

It was very peaceful in the orchard. The small noises seemed to be magnified by the stillness of the morning. There was a steady munching as Muffin cropped the grass, and the gentle crooning and clucking of the hens as they wandered about the grass, pecking and investigating. From all around came the sound of birds, singing to the morning, and in the distance the whirring of some farm vehicle. This can't be happening, Jess thought to herself, stroking Polly's tense neck and noticing that the pony's grey coat was darkening with sweat. Polly can't be ill. Not Polly, who jumped at loud noises and shied and snorted at almost everything, when she was in that sort of mood. Jess talked to her pony, anything that came into her mind. She told her how lovely she was. She told her about the riding club meeting. About the holidays that would begin on Thursday. And Polly just stood there, stiff and unresponsive.

"Mr Warburton's coming straight away." Mum arrived by Jess's side, slipping an arm around her, comfortingly, and looking at Polly with troubled eyes. "Is this how she is all the time?" she asked.

Jess nodded, tears welling in her eyes. "It looks bad, doesn't it, Mum?" she said.

"It doesn't look good," her mother agreed, "but let's wait for the vet. No good to get yourself too upset."

Jess swallowed hard. "I don't like to try and move her," she told her mother, "I'll wait until— "

"Oh! There he is now! Goodness, he wasn't long!"

Mr Warburton hurried down the path towards the orchard, followed by Dad and Tommy.

They all gathered around Polly. Mr Warburton,

after a curt nod of greeting, examined the pony carefully. He looked at her eyes, felt her neck and down her legs. After a short time, he turned to Jess. "It's bad, Jess," he said, gently. He included the whole of the family when he spoke again. Kim and Clare, jeans and sweaters pulled hastily over their pyjamas, had also arrived. The Caswell family, together, had never been so silent.

"Unless I'm very much mistaken," Mr Warburton said, quietly, "Polly has tetanus. Has she been injected against tetanus, Jess?" he asked. Jess shook her head. "I don't know," she admitted. "I've only had her since Christmas. I didn't know about injections against things . . ."

"Well, it doesn't really matter, now," Mr Warburton continued. He bent down and opened his bag. "I'll take a blood sample and test it, but for now we must assume that Polly has tetanus."

"But tetanus," Dad began. "That's very serious. She could—"

He stopped, not wanting to upset Jess, but Mr Warburton finished his sentence for him. "Yes, Mr Caswell, she could, and probably *will* die, I'm afraid. I'm sorry, Jess," he added quickly, turning to her, "but I must say it straight away. Really, I ought to advise you to let me put Polly—"

"*No!*" Until now, Jess had found it difficult to speak, but now she almost shouted. "No! You can't put her down!" She looked frantically at

166

her mother and father. "We can't, can we? Not Polly!"

"Jess, if it's really as bad as that," Mrs Caswell said, "We must listen to what Mr Warburton says— "

"You see, Jess," the vet interrupted, "there is an eighty per cent mortality rate with tetanus."

"What does that mean?" Jess asked miserably.

"Nearly all ponies and horses with tetanus – eighty per cent of them – die. We just can't save them. I can *try*," he added, "but you must realise that it is very unlikely that Polly will recover. And," he added, turning to Jess's parents, "treating her will be very expensive."

Dad spoke quietly. "If you think there's any chance at all," he said, "just go ahead. We'll foot the bill. But we don't want Polly to suffer, do we, Jess?" he added gently to his daughter.

Jess shook her head, and then buried her face in Polly's long mane, letting the tears come. But she didn't cry for long.

"Come on then, Jess." Mr Warburton spoke quietly but firmly. "You must try to lead Polly over towards the gate." He turned to Mr Caswell, "Have you got straw?"

"I'm not sure— " Mr Caswell began, but his wife interrupted.

"Yes! Plenty of it. Jess got it in case we had a really bad winter and she had to keep the ponies in."

"Good," said Mr Warburton, snapping shut his case having taken the blood sample. "We must get moving straight away. No time to lose. Straw down in the stable and some extra bales – at least twelve, if possible."

Chapter 9

It was much better being busy, Jess discovered. She didn't have time to cry, or feel miserable. There was plenty to do. While Mum, Dad and the two girls went ahead to prepare the stable, Jess and Tommy began the slow journey with Polly.

"Come on, Polly. Come on, girl," Jess encouraged, pulling gently at Polly's halter.

Tommy, on the other side of the grey mare, encouraged her, too. "Polly, *poor* Polly," he murmured, reaching up to stroke the mare's sweating neck.

Slowly, oh, so slowly, the pony made her way stiffly towards the gate, one step at a time. Every movement seemed so difficult. All the time, Jess talked to her, soothing talk about anything and everything. Polly knew Jess's voice well, and Jess hoped that somehow hearing her would help. She wondered if the pony *could* hear her. She asked Mr Warburton, who had just come back from fetching a syringe from his car.

"Oh, yes," he said. "She can hear all right." They were in the stable, with Polly standing in a deep bedding of straw. "In fact," Mr Warburton added, "one of my next jobs will be to put pieces of cotton wool in both her ears."

"Why?" Jess asked.

"Because all noises will upset her. Everything around her must be as quiet as possible," Mr Warburton explained. "You must tell everyone in the family to be especially quiet around the stable."

"I have to give her an antitoxin now," he added. "She's going to have quite a few injections, I'm afraid, and she's also going to need antibiotics and muscle-relaxants." He smiled briefly at Jess. "I'll do my best, Jess, but I can't make any promises," he told her, gently. "You're going to have a lot to do, too," he added, as he prepared to give the first injection.

"What can I do now?" Jess asked.

"Yes, what can we do, Mr Warburton?" Mrs Caswell said, appearing at their side.

"Those bales of straw," Mr Warburton replied. "When I've finished with my injections, I want them packed up against Polly. One of the most important things to avoid," he explained, "is Polly going down."

"Falling on to the ground you mean?"

"That's it. If that happens, well . . . " Mr Warburton didn't have to finish his sentence.

Working quietly, and talking with lowered voices, the family packed the bales around the immobile body of Polly. She stood, her legs extended, stiff and straight. Her head pointed forward, and her ears, now filled with large wads of cotton wool, were permanently pricked. She was sweating, and occasionally she shuddered as a spasm passed over her.

"Now," Mr Warburton instructed, beckoning them to the door, "we must let her be quiet." He looked round at them all, his face serious. "You must be quiet at all times. No banging of doors. No shouting." He looked across at the orchard, where Muffin was watching from the gate. "And I should find somewhere for the other pony, for now, just in case he starts to miss Polly and begins whinnying. And check that he has had his anti-tetanus injection."

"I'll ring Mrs Carter," Mum told Jess, "I'm sure she won't mind having Muffin back, just until . . . until . . . " Mrs Caswell faltered. Mr Warburton had told them quite clearly that there was little hope for Polly.

"Until Polly gets better," Jess said fiercely.

"Jess, you mustn't hope too much," her mother said, her eyes worried.

"It's all right, Mum," Jess said, quietly. "I won't. But I'm not going to think about Polly dying," she added stubbornly. "I *can't*." She looked up at her mother, her eyes dark with pain. "I just can't," she repeated. "But I'm not stupid. I know it may happen, but while Polly's still alive . . . "

171

"Yes, dear, I understand. Well, I'll go and ring Mrs Carter and then I'll arrange for a horse-box." Gradually, the family drifted away, Mum to telephone, Tommy to collect Muffin from the field and to take him well away from the stable. Dad had to go to work that morning, and on his way he was dropping Clare at her ballet class.

It was Kim who asked Mr Warburton about food for Polly. "She can't move her mouth much, can she?" she said.

"That's right," Mr Warburton replied. "She can't chew or swallow properly, so she can't eat in the normal way. What you can do," he continued, turning to Jess, "is offer her water. Try and get her to drink, somehow. And you may be able to get something down her – perhaps some baby food, or some invalid food." Jess looked uncertain, and he continued, "Spoon it down, if you can, through the side of her mouth where the gap is between her front and back teeth. Anything, just to give her some nourishment." He pushed his fingers through his hair in agitation. "Now, I must get back to my surgery. But I'll be back later on today and I'll see if I can fix something up – some kind of a drip – so that she can have nourishment. See you later, Jess."

Jess was alone. She was alone with the terrifying thought of what might be going to happen. Very quietly, she pushed open the door of the stable and slipped in. She stood a few feet away

172

from Polly who stood immobile, looking like the wooden horse of Troy.

Then Polly had a spasm. Her whole body shuddered, and her grey coat darkened even more with sweat. Feeling useless and wretched, Jess turned away. She must *do* something. The baby food. She must go and buy some and try to get some down Polly's throat. And she must telephone Beckie. The riding club meeting was at Beckie's house today but Jess felt detached from all thoughts of the riding club – in fact, she had forgotten all about it until now. She looked at her watch: it was only twenty past nine and yet Jess felt as if she had been up all day.

"Beckie?"

"Jess! Oughtn't you to be on your way by now?"

Jess swallowed hard. Words wouldn't seem to come to her mouth. They were stuck somewhere in her throat, together with an awful desire to howl with misery.

"Jess?" This time Beckie's voice sounded worried. "Is something wrong?"

Jess swallowed again, gulping down the misery with an effort. "Beckie . . . " she began, her voice no more than a croaky whisper, "it's Polly."

Knowing Jess so well, Beckie knew instantly that it was serious. "Is she – is it— " she stammered.

"Tetanus," Jess croaked.

"That's bad, isn't it?" Not waiting for a reply, Beckie continued in a rush, "Jess, I'm coming over, straight away."

"But the riding club—" Jess began to protest, finding her voice at last.

"Oh, blow the riding club!" Beckie replied. "I'll leave a message with Mum."

"Beckie?"

"Yes?"

"There mustn't be noise. We all have to be quiet. Better walk Justin when you get near."

"I'll get Dad to bring me," Beckie said, quickly. "I'll be there as soon as I can." The line went dead. Despite her misery Jess found herself smiling. When Beckie decided to act, she didn't hang around!

Chapter 10

"I can hardly believe it *is* Polly out there in the stable," Beckie said. After visiting Polly and watching Jess attempt to spoon baby food into her mouth, Beckie had been glad to come indoors with Jess.

Every few moments, Jess thought of her wooden horse, standing in the straw, but it was good to be away from the stable for a bit.

"When I think," Jess began, "how I was always telling her that she was too lively— "

"Don't!" said Beckie. She gazed into the fire. "If only I could *do* something," she said. She thumped the arm of her wheelchair angrily. "But I'm so *useless* like this."

"But you *are* doing something."

"I don't see how. I couldn't help you just now, could I, in the stable? All *I* could do was watch while you tried to feed Polly."

"But there isn't much anyone can do," Jess told her, "and I'm really glad you're here." Her hand slipped down to stroke Badger's black and white head as he leant against her leg. Jess looked across at Beckie. "You know that Polly will probably die?" she asked, surprised at how calm her voice was.

Beckie nodded. "I'm sorry, Jess," she said, miserably. "It's all my fault."

"Beckie, how *could* it be?"

Beckie ran her finger around the rim of her mug and looked down as she spoke. "I should have known about the anti-tetanus injection. I *should* have. I bet all the others know – Rachel and Sam and— "

"Well, *I* didn't know, either."

"Well, we're both hopeless, aren't we? Sorry," Beckie added, grinning sheepishly at her friend. "I'm not being much of a comfort, am I?"

"Let's look it up in my *Horse Keeper's Guide*," Jess suggested, "I'll fetch it from my bedroom."

The book proved to be of little help. "All it says," Jess said, "is 'For all wounds, however slight, get your vet to give the horse an anti-tetanus injection as soon as possible.'"

"Did Polly have a cut?" Beckie asked.

Jess shook her head. "I wish she had," she said miserably. "I would have called Mr Warburton and then she would have had the injection and perhaps she wouldn't have had tetanus." Jess closed the book. "This doesn't do any good," she said, "I'd better go back and have a look at her."

Beckie stayed until Mr Warburton had called again. He came in the afternoon, armed with wires, tubes and bottles.

176

"I don't suppose you've got electricity in the stable?" the vet asked. Jess shook her head. "I didn't think you would," he continued, "so I brought a car battery. I've got this special attachment, you see," he added. "It's useful in this sort of case."

"That's for the drip, is it?" Jess asked.

"That's right," Mr Warburton replied. "I'll set it all up outside, and I'll go in quietly and fix it up. Then I'll show you how to work it." He looked across at Jess quickly. "I'd better show your mum, too," he said, "since this is going to need at least two people. The bottles will have to be changed every few hours, day and night."

An uneasy silence settled around Trumpeter Cottage. Even the paper-boy, who had been told of Polly's illness and who was reminded daily by the large notice which Jess had fixed to the gate, walked carefully down the path without his usual whistle, and closed the gate carefully and quietly behind him.

Jess changed the bottles, offered Polly fresh water regularly, kept the stable as clean and fresh as possible, and watched as her pony became daily thinner and weaker. Nobody mentioned school when Monday came. Miss Claremont telephoned on Monday evening. "Don't worry about school," she said. "We won't be doing anything very important before the end of term. And, Jess . . . "

Jess waited, half her thoughts with Polly and the next change of bottles. "I don't want to give you too much hope," Miss Claremont continued, "but I do remember a pony that recovered. It belonged to a friend of mine."

Jess clung to that thought as she looked at Polly's thin body, standing stiffly in the stable. It was dark and she and Mrs Caswell worked in silence, Jess holding the torch and Mum renewing the liquid in the bottle.

"She looks worse, Mum." Jess allowed a tear to trickle down her cheek when they were in the darkness outside the stable, leaving Polly alone inside.

"It's only three days, love," Mrs Caswell reminded her, putting a comforting arm around her shoulders. "We can't expect miracles. At least she's still alive."

Jess found this phrase a useful one to say when people telephoned – Rachel, Sam, Jackie and Dawn.

"She's still alive," Jess said, feeling unreal as she spoke. "She's just the same. No improvement. But she's still alive." She wanted to shout with anger, cry with misery. It was like some terrible, never-ending nightmare. And in some ways, Jess did not want this nightmare to end – unless she could choose the ending.

Anna came over on the Friday afternoon. She stood awkwardly in the hall, clutching a plastic bag.

"I couldn't think of anything else to bring you," she said, pulling out some pony magazines. "Oh, Jess!" she burst out. "I'm so sorry! It's terrible. But – but, she's still— "

"Yes," Jess replied, automatically, "she's still alive."

"No . . . no, I mean— " Anna bit her lip. "Oh dear, I don't want to raise your hopes, but . . . "

"What is it, Anna?"

"Well, I read up tetanus in a magazine and it said how serious it is, and everything, and how the pony usually dies, but . . . well, it said that the pony generally dies within three to five days."

It took a moment for Anna's words to register. Then Jess's heart lurched with excitement. "You mean, if she's alive now, maybe she's going to get better?"

Anna nodded. "It's in one of those magazines," she said, pointing to the bundle in Jess's arms. "I thought you might like to read about it. Well, I wasn't sure, really, whether you'd want to or not," she admitted.

Jess waited impatiently for Mr Warburton's next visit. He had called twice a day since Polly had been taken ill. He was delayed on Friday evening,

180

and did not arrive until nearly eight o'clock. Jess, sitting in the deep recess of the hall window with Dandy curled on her lap, was nearly asleep when the lights of the vet's car shone down the drive. Sending an indignant cat hurtling to the ground, Jess was quickly through the front door to meet him.

"What is it, Jess? Is there some improvement?" Mr Warburton asked, seeing Jess's excited face.

Jess shook her head. "No," she admitted, "but . . ."

As they walked slowly towards the stable, she told him about the article, and he nodded. He stopped outside the shed. "Yes, Jess," he said, quietly. "It's true that since Polly is still with us, there *is* some hope. But," he added, as her eyes shone, "you must realise that she is getting weaker all the time, and if she goes down . . ."

"Yes, I know." Jess, duly sobered, quietly pushed open the door of the stable. After Mr Warburton's words, she hardly dared to look. But Polly was still standing. Everything was still the same . . . but something was different, wasn't it? At the time, Jess couldn't think what it was, but afterwards she realised that the cotton wool had fallen out of Polly's left ear.

All at once, Jess felt very tired. Polly was still standing, as she had done for nearly a week. Was it ever going to end? As she and Mr

Warburton stepped forward towards the pony, Mr Warburton suddenly stopped and grabbed Jess's arm. "Look!" he hissed. "Look at her ear!"

At the sound of their approach, Polly's ear had twitched back, just a little. But just a little was enough to set Jess's heart racing. She looked at Mr Warburton and there was definitely hope in his eyes. "Is she . . . is she getting better?" Jess breathed.

The vet stepped forward eagerly. "Well, Jess," he said, turning back towards her momentarily, "I won't make any promises, but that's a very hopeful sign. Let's have a look at her!"

But there was no need. The next moment, Jess heard the sound that she had thought she might never hear again. Hearing Jess's voice, Polly turned her head slightly – and a little stiffly – and whickered. It was a soft, throaty whicker, and it sent tears careering down Jess's cheeks. In a moment, Jess was by her pony, her arms around the mare's neck, which was still tense and slightly damp with sweat but which now felt like a real flesh-and-blood neck and not one belonging to a wooden horse.

"Polly, Polly." Jess sobbed, and that was all she could say.

Mr Warburton left her alone, and quietly felt Polly all over. At last he put an arm on Jess's shoulder. "It's leaving her, Jess," he said, triumphantly. "We're very, very lucky. The stiffness is going. She'll be able to move properly very soon."

Still with her arms around the pony's neck, Jess turned towards Mr Warburton, the tears of happiness still on her cheeks. "Oh, thank you!" she said.

"Don't thank me," Mr Warburton said simply. "If Polly had had a very bad dose, nothing we could have done would have saved her. But as it is," he added, "I think that you and your family have done a lot towards Polly's recovery. If you hadn't looked after her like you did, then maybe she wouldn't have recovered." He reached for his veterinary bag. "But come on, Jess, we've got plenty to do now!" Jess looked at him enquiringly. "Food!" he pronounced. "That's what she's going to need. Very carefully at first – little and often." He grinned at Jess and added, "Now you're really going to have to work hard!"

Chapter 11

It wasn't how she had imagined spending the Easter holidays, but Jess was not grumbling. Beckie, the first person outside the Caswell family to be told of Polly's recovery and to visit her in the stable, spread the news to the other members of the riding club. Soon a string of visitors arrived at Trumpeter Cottage.

"I think I might as well put up a sign at the gate, offering coffee and teas!" Mrs Caswell commented, after one particularly busy morning when Sam and Rachel had arrived at almost the same time, closely followed by Dawn and Jackie. "I might be able to make some money for the Caswell family's dwindling resources!" she added cheerfully.

Guilt spread through Jess as she remembered Mr Warburton's words when he had first told them that Polly had tetanus. "Treating her will be very expensive," he had said.

"Mum!" Jess looked at her mother anxiously. "What's it going to cost, Polly's illness? Mr Warburton's been coming twice a day for a week, and he's still coming. And all those injections."

"We'll manage, love." Mrs Caswell smiled across at her. "We always do! The loveliest thing is to see Polly looking stronger every day."

That was true, Jess thought as she watched Polly eating her food, a little while later. Polly was very thin, but already, after only a few days of feeding, she was beginning to fill out, just a little. Her beautiful arab head, which turned every time Jess entered the stable, was even finer. Now she was able to move around freely in the stable, and Mr Warburton pronounced her completely free of the poisoning effect of the tetanus. "Plenty of love and care," he said, "and she'll be back to her old fitness in no time. But," he added, "I wouldn't ride her for a while. Perhaps just a little ride at the end of the holidays, if all goes to plan."

"You can ride Justin," Beckie said over the telephone.

"But I don't mind not riding," Jess protested. "As long as Polly's better, I just don't care."

"Oh, go on," Beckie urged. "I'd love to know what you think of him. Carol says he's lovely to ride – bouncy and ponyish."

"Well . . . maybe . . . "

"This afternoon?" Beckie always liked to do things straight away. "Your mum will feed Polly, won't she?"

"Yes, I'm sure she will."

* * *

Jess couldn't remember the last time she had cycled over to Beckie's house. It seemed strange to be bumping along through the lanes on her old bike instead of riding Polly. She couldn't see over the hedges so easily – but at least the bike didn't shy at anything, Jess thought with a grin. She had to admit that it felt marvellous to be out after spending her time either in Polly's stable or in the house worrying, or grabbing a hasty snack or quick snooze.

Beckie was waiting at the gate. "What kept you?" she demanded, whirling her chair around and hurrying towards the stable. Justin was waiting, saddled and bridled and ready for off. Jess propped her bicycle against the side of the stable. Beckie seemed very cheerful, she thought. "I tacked him up," Beckie said, proudly.

"What – even the saddle?" Jess asked.

"Yes. He's so good."

"But," Jess looked puzzled, "surely you couldn't reach to put the saddle on his back?"

Beckie grinned. "Well, Jess Caswell, just you watch this," she said, mysteriously. Beckie wheeled herself over towards the door. She pushed down the flap of her foot rest, so that her feet touched the ground. Then, pushing against the stable door with her right hand and hanging on to the chair with her left, she raised herself up until she was standing. She wobbled a little precariously, and her back was bent over, but she was able to reach to the height of Justin's back.

"The saddle was on the top of the lower door, you see," she explained, "and I could slide it onto his back. I could only do it because he's so good," she added. She grinned. "I couldn't have saddled Polly!" Her smile faded, and she looked serious. "I felt so hopeless, Jess, that day when I came over – when Polly was first ill. I told Dr James about it." She smiled again. "He said, 'Well, why don't you start trying to stand up?'"

"But you can't— "

"No, I know I can't walk. But Dr James has been giving me all these extra exercises. He says I must try to stand somehow, just to strengthen my legs, even if my back isn't quite— "

"But will you be able to walk?" Jess interrupted, eagerly.

Beckie shook her head, and her eyes looked pained – almost frightened, Jess thought. "I just don't know," she admitted, "and Dr James doesn't know either. He seems to think, now, that my back is basically just weak, but not permanently damaged. All he'll say these days," Beckie concluded, wryly, "is 'we'll see', and— "

"But that's really amazing!" Jess broke in. "Remember, that's what Mr Warburton said about Polly – and look at her now! Anyway, do you realise," she added, as she checked the girth on Justin's saddle, "that I've never seen you standing before?"

187

Beckie was back in her wheelchair, looking strained, so Jess tactfully changed the subject. "Right then, Justin," she said, addressing the sturdy black pony, "you're going to give me my first ride for nearly two weeks!" Justin flicked back one ear and stood quite still while Jess mounted. Settling herself into the saddle, and adjusting the stirrups, Jess reported to Beckie, "He feels ever so comfortable – like sitting in an armchair!"

"Where will you ride him?" asked Beckie, the pride of ownership shining in her eyes, now, and her other problems temporarily forgotten.

"It's not far to the common from here. OK if I take him up there?"

Justin had a shorter stride than Polly, Jess discovered. His high-stepping trot took some getting used to, but as they reached the gateway leading into the northern end of the common, Jess was beginning to enjoy her ride immensely. Justin was eager and keen to go, but his training stopped him from changing to a canter until instructed.

As Jess squeezed him with her legs, and as he changed his gait to a smooth, flowing canter, Jess remembered that other day on the common. It was less than two months since Jess and Polly had ridden over the short grass there, on that blustery, sunny day of last term, but to Jess it seemed like a lifetime away. She thought of

Polly, back in her stable, eating her meal and gradually gaining strength, and her heart filled with thankfulness that Polly was alive. The sun even managed to break through the grey clouds, turning the sombre green of the common to sparkling gold. Everything was wonderful, Jess thought, except . . . As she watched Justin's long black mane bouncing on his neck, and felt his smooth canter, Jess thought of Beckie. It was Beckie who ought to be up here on Justin's back. That was the only thing wrong, now, in Jess's life. If only Beckie could walk and run and ride, just like any normal person. If only . . .

"What was he like?" Beckie demanded, when they returned.

"Great!" Jess told her. "His trot's bouncy, but his canter's smooth." She laughed. "And he behaves so well! I'm used to Polly jumping and spooking all the time!" Quickly, Jess remembered. "Still, I wouldn't have her any other way," she added, sliding down from Justin's saddle, and patting his warm neck.

"When Polly's really better," Beckie said, reaching up to stroke Justin, "we'll go for a ride, shall we? Just a quiet one, because she won't be feeling strong. I'll take Justin and the trap and you ride Polly."

"OK," Jess said, "before the end of the holidays. Just a quiet ride."

Chapter 12

Jess had asked Mr Warburton and he had agreed. The Easter holidays were nearly over and Polly was back in the orchard, enjoying the spring grass with Muffin, who had returned eagerly from his brief holiday with the Carters. Polly looked fit and well: she had filled out, and was perhaps even a little fatter than before her illness. Her thick winter coat was coming out at a fast rate, leaving a covering of grey hair on the cobbles each time Jess groomed her.

"Her muscles just need toning up a bit," the vet told Jess. "Walking, and some gentle trotting for a while, and perhaps some hill work. She'll soon be back to normal."

Now that the day had come, Jess found herself shaking slightly with excitement as she gathered up the reins, put her left foot in the stirrup and jumped into the saddle. She laughed out loud as Polly jogged on the spot, chewing on her snaffle bit and tossing her head. "She's just the same," she told Tommy, who was watching from the orchard gate, from where an interested Muffin watched, too.

"She looks much nicer like that," Tommy

said, stoically, "than standing all stiff in the stable."

Jess grinned across at her small brother. "You've never said truer words, Tommy," she told him, squeezing Polly slightly with her heels, and feeling the pony move away down the path. "See you later," she called, "Won't be long – it's only going to be a quiet ride."

Polly greeted Justin like a long-lost friend. The two met at the crossroads, just outside Edgecombe.

"Where shall we go?" Beckie asked from the trap. Justin stood, solid and square between the shafts. Polly, excited by her first outing for many weeks, moved restlessly on the spot, snorting at Justin and swinging her head to listen to every sound around her.

"Polly's winter coat has almost gone," Beckie added. "She looks really lovely, Jess. You would never think she'd been so ill."

Jess smoothed the silky grey neck. "She seems to have plenty of energy," she said. "How about going down Holder's Lane, along the valley, up past the common and onto the coast road?" she suggested. "Mr Warburton said I should give her some hill work to strengthen her muscles."

"OK. Justin likes it up there." Beckie laughed. "He seems to like the smell of the sea!" She shook the reins and called to Justin to "move on".

191

The lane was narrow and steep so Jess rode ahead on Polly, who danced sideways down the road while Justin followed more slowly.

"She just won't walk," Jess called back over her shoulder.

"Never mind, she'll quieten down when we get to Valley Road," Beckie said.

The lane began to widen, and as the girls reached the left-hand bend on the road, they heard the steady roar of a tractor coming up the hill. Sensing a chance to show off, Polly stopped, with high-flung head and dilated nostrils, as the tractor and heavily laden trailer rounded the bend. Taff Collins from Edgecombe Farm waved cheerily from the seat of his vehicle.

"Mornin'," he called. "Lovely day!" He nodded in Polly's direction, as he added, "See she's none the worse for her illness!"

Jess smiled at the farmer. "It's her first day out!" she called.

Tractor and trailer forgotten, Polly moved on down the hill, prancing and snorting at anything and everything.

Jess turned in the saddle to grin at her friend. "She really is— " Jess began. But Beckie never did hear the end of Jess's sentence, for at that moment Polly saw something flutter in the verge. She shot across the road to the other side, where the trailer had dropped some mud on the road on its way up the hill.

Horrified, Beckie watched as Polly slipped on the mud and then fell sideways, taking Jess with her. For a moment, Jess was pinned to the ground by the pony's weight. Then Polly scrambled awkwardly to her feet and trotted on down the road, frightened and confused by the fall but not injured by it.

Beckie looked at Jess. She was lying in the road. Jess raised herself up on one elbow.

"Jess! Are you all right?"

"I . . . I don't know. I . . . feel . . . " Jess moved slightly and cried out in pain. "I think I've done something to my leg," she called, weakly.

Beckie was just about to yell to Jess that she was going for help when she heard a shout.

"Look out!" a voice called from higher up the hill. Beckie heard a low rumbling noise, and her heart began to pound, for she knew instinctively what it must be. As her brain worked it out, her eyes saw the trailer, parted from the tractor, careering down the hill towards the opposite side of the road – towards Jess!

Jess heard the sound, but she couldn't work out what it was. Her hat had fallen off, and her head hurt where it had come into contact with the road. Her leg hurt a lot, and she didn't want to move. She would just lie there until someone came to help them. Was Polly all right? she wondered. Then, suddenly, she found herself

being picked up by the shoulders and dragged across the road. She cried out in pain. Why didn't whoever it was leave her there? It hurt being moved. She turned her head slightly and saw Beckie sitting beside her. How did Beckie get to be out in the road with her? Jess thought vaguely, before she passed out and as the trailer thundered past, its huge wheel passing within an inch of her broken leg.

Jess watched across the top of her plastered leg as nurses flitted past, hurrying up and down the long ward. She thought about Polly. Was she all right after her fall? And what about the vet's bill? Jess wondered, her mind jumping to another worry. It seemed to be a long time since Polly's illness, and yet the dreaded bill had still not arrived. She asked her mother about it when she came in to see her.

"Ah, well . . . " Mrs Caswell said, mysteriously. "That's been paid."

Jess hardly dared to ask, but she did. "How much was it?" she said.

"I don't know," Mum replied, smiling enigmatically.

"But, Mum, you must— "

"Jess." Mum spoke firmly. "You're supposed to be resting. Remember, you had slight concussion. Otherwise you'd be up and about on that leg by now, plaster or no plaster!"

"But, Mum," Jess began again. Really Mum was exasperating sometimes.

Mrs Caswell leaned forward and smiled again. "It's all taken care of, Jessie," she explained. "Mr Warburton rang me up and told me it had been paid – anonymously." "But of course," she added, "we all know who paid it."

"Beckie's parents! But that's not fair, Mum. I know Beckie said she felt it was her fault that Polly contracted tetanus because she hadn't had her injected against it, but that's ridiculous. *I* should have known about the anti-tetanus injection."

"I know, love. I agree with you. I went round to see Mrs Stockwood. But when I saw Beckie . . . well, I understood."

Jess looked at her mother in disbelief. "Well, *I* don't understand," she complained. We can't let them pay . . . "

"It's just their way of showing their gratitude – to someone. Maybe even to Polly," said Mrs Caswell.

Jess leaned back on her pillows. "Mum. I must be still suffering from concussion," she said, closing her eyes. "I don't know *what* you're talking about!"

"You don't remember much about your accident, do you?" Mum asked.

Jess opened her eyes again and looked across at her mother. "I do . . . a bit," she said, slowly. "I

196

can remember Polly falling . . . and then . . . being pulled across the road and my leg hurting. That's about it."

"You don't know who pulled you – and probably saved your life, or at least saved you from much worse injury – from the trailer?"

"Oh, yes . . . the trailer. I remember hearing something. It must have been the trailer." Jess turned puzzled eyes towards her mother. "*Who* saved me, Mum? I don't understand. What has it got to do with the Stockwoods paying the vet's bill?"

"Ah, there she is now," said Mrs Caswell, looking towards the door. Jess followed her gaze and stared in disbelief. It couldn't be – but it was. Beckie was coming through the doorway, grinning broadly. But she wasn't sitting in her wheelchair. She was walking – a little stiffly, and with the aid of a stick, admittedly, but she was *walking!*

Chapter 13

The horse's head drawn in Biro on Jess's plaster cast looked very much like Polly's, Jess decided. Those small, pointed ears and that neat dished face with big eyes and such a long wispy mane had to belong to beautiful, gorgeous Polly. Besides, Beckie had drawn it! While she was drawing, Beckie had explained about wanting to try to walk when Dr James had encouraged her to have a go. But she had been afraid – afraid that she wouldn't be able to and that she would just fall in a heap on the ground. Then, that day of the ride when she had seen the runaway trailer hurtling down towards Jess, she had known that it was time to do it – to walk. And Beckie had known that she *must* walk. As Beckie put it, "There wasn't any maybe about it – I knew I *would* walk." She laughed. "Actually, I *ran*!" she said. She looked up from her drawing, her eyes dancing with happiness. "I shan't need the stick soon," she told Jess. "Dr James says I'll be walking so well soon that no one will ever guess that once I was in a wheelchair." She looked down at the blue Biro drawing of Polly, which gazed back at her from Jess's plaster.

"And you know, Jess," she said, "it's all because of Polly."

Jess tilted her head on one side questioningly. "Well, you see," Beckie explained, "if Polly hadn't been ill, she probably wouldn't have fallen, and then if she hadn't fallen and broken your leg, I might never have *tried* to walk!"

"I think you would have – eventually," Jess said.

"Well, *I* think it was all Polly's doing," Beckie replied firmly. Her eyes danced again as she looked across at her friend. "And now I'll be able to ride Justin," she said happily.

When Beckie had gone, Jess leaned back in her bed and sighed with happiness. She forgot that she was in hospital. What did that matter? After all, Polly was alive and fit and waiting in the orchard at home, and Beckie could walk.

Jess wriggled as her leg itched under the plaster. Of course, there *was* the leg. She wouldn't be able to ride for at least six weeks. "Oh, well," she told herself, sighing, "you can't have everything in this life." Jess gazed at the sketch on her plaster and smiled. "Just you wait," she whispered to the drawing, "until the summer holidays. Just wait, Polly . . . "

ON
LOCATION

Chapter 1

It was hot. In fact, it was *too* hot Jess decided, stretching out her bare legs further into the cool grass.

Jessica Caswell wriggled a little so that her back rested more comfortably against the trunk of the old apple tree. She didn't really mind if the others did not come just yet. In fact, Jess wanted to be by herself. She wanted to think things out. But, after all, she argued back at herself, there wasn't much to think out, was there?

A long, contented snort made Jess turn her head, and reminded her that she should be thinking about grooming Polly and saddling her. The other members of Edgecombe Valley Riding Club would be here soon.

Jess could see most of the orchard from her horizontal position, but the snort had come from behind the shed. Then she appeared – the pony of Jess's dreams, and now also of her waking life – her head lowered as she sniffed at the grass before cropping it. Jess watched her pony with pride. She noted the fine, clear-cut features of Polly's grey arab head; the thin, wispy forelock and mane which hung delicately about her broad forehead and slender neck; her fine legs and long, banner tail.

"Hello, Polly girl," Jess called, lazily.

Polly snorted again, coming closer to peer at her lethargic owner. The grey arab looming above her looked like a giant horse, Jess thought. And even fat little Muffin, wandering in Polly's wake, looked much larger than his twelve hands. Muffin did not belong to Jess but was on loan from the Carters, who lived in the next village. Jess looked after Muffin and sometimes took Tommy, her young brother, for a ride on him.

As the two ponies turned away, Jess closed her eyes and allowed herself to soak up the pleasure of the moment; July at Trumpeter Cottage, wonderful weather, Polly fit and well again, and the first day of the summer holidays.

Jess's mind wandered back to her earlier worry. Why couldn't Beckie and Rachel get on together? When Beckie had been confined to a wheelchair, things hadn't been so bad, but now that she was mobile again, the two of them were always arguing – always at each others' throats. It was beginning to disrupt the meetings of the recently formed riding club.

Jess sighed. Why did life always have to be complicated, she wondered? Why did there have to be this problem, just as everything seemed to be perfect, with Polly completely well after her terrible illness, Beckie out of her wheelchair and walking, and Jess herself able to ride again now that her broken leg was mended ...

"So *that*'s where you're hiding!"

Jess flicked open her eyes. Twelve-year-old Beckie stood above her, looking hot and a trifle indignant. Her face was streaked with sweat and strands of dark hair from her fringe clung to her forehead.

"I didn't hear you come," said Jess.

"I left Justin in the shade by your gate," Beckie explained, sitting down beside her friend. "You're not ready," she added, accusingly.

"You're early," Jess retorted mildly. She giggled. "You sound like my mother," she added. Then, feeling sorry for her hot friend, she handed her the flask which lay beside her in the grass. "Have some," she offered. "It's lemon squash – with ice."

"Thanks," Beckie Stockwood poured herself

some squash, drinking it down in one gulp. "That was brilliant," she said, lying back full-length in the grass. She pushed back her sticky fringe. "It's much too hot to do *anything*," she stated.

"Even ride."

They were silent for a few minutes, considering this amazing fact. Beckie broke the silence. "You're quiet today," she told her friend, turning her head sideways to view Jess quizzically.

"Mmm."

"Anything wrong?"

"No . . . not really." Jess hesitated. She wondered if perhaps she could broach the subject now. "It's just—" she began. But suddenly the two girls were surrounded by noisy chatter and any number of legs as Rachel, Samantha and Richard arrived together, accompanied by Richard's long-legged lurcher dog Columbus, who was young, exuberant and always getting in the way.

Everyone flopped at the same time. There was an unspoken agreement to postpone the riding club outing until the hottest hour of the day had passed. Dawn and Jackie arrived, closely followed by Anna, and they joined the others on the grass. For a while there was

silence as they savoured the relative coolness beneath the trees.

"Pity there's no pond here," Sam remarked, lying back in the cool grass. "I'd jump in if there was!"

Richard Orley, resting against one of the apple trees, said, "How about the river – it's quite wide in places."

"You know, Richie," said Sam, sitting up and looking across at him wickedly, "Just occasionally you say something almost intelligent!" She ducked as he threw a stick at her. Then, standing up and addressing the gathering she added, "Come on, you lot. Let's head for the river!"

"But we're all dressed for riding," Anna pointed out sensibly.

"I'm all right," Richard said. Richard, who lived in a caravan with his unconventional writer and artist parents, always rode bareback on his big bay cob, Crusader, and so was dressed today in shorts and a T-shirt.

"And I've got shorts in my rucksack," said Sam.

"Well, I'm not going," said Beckie. "My jodhpurs take ages to dry."

"Really!" Rachel looked across at her scornfully as she spoke. "Trust you!"

Beckie glared back and was about to comment, but Jess saved the situation. "Don't worry," she put in hastily, "I'm sure I can find enough shorts and things for the rest of us. I'll sneak out some of Clare's. She's got loads."

The swim temporarily washed away any tension. In actual fact, no one swam – the water-level was too low in the river – but everyone managed to get very wet, and a lot of laughter floated up from the reedy little river. After half an hour of hilarity, eight wet, two-legged figures made their way back to Trumpeter Cottage, accompanied by a very wet and bedraggled four-legged one.

"Good heavens!" Jess's mother, emerging from the back door of the cottage, viewed them with amusement. "I never know what this riding club will get up to next," she laughed. "What have you been doing – trying to drown poor Columbus? Did you tell them, Jess?" she added, turning to her daughter.

"No, I forgot," Jess admitted. "Got some news," she informed her companions. "Tell you what," she added, "let's have our picnic now, in the orchard, instead of on the ride. We can dry off in the sun, and it'll be cooler for the ride."

"What about the news?" asked Beckie.
"Tell you in the orchard!"

Chapter 2

"When?"

"How long for?"

"Who told you?"

Jess took another bite of her sandwich and chewed, annoyingly slowly, before answering the barrage of questions through a mouthful of egg and cress.

"Mrs Hasty at the post office told me," she explained. "She knows *everything* about *everyone*! They'll be there about a month," Jess continued, swallowing her mouthful and looking round at her audience. "And I think they're there already," she added. "The director, or somebody, has been to the post office and told Mrs Hasty all about it."

"It might be fun." Beckie's voice was a shade doubtful.

"It *will* be fun," Jess replied firmly. "There might be work for us, too!"

"Work? What – acting?" Beckie queried.

"They'll have their own actors," Rachel said, her voice scornful.

Jess continued excitedly. "They might want helpers, Mrs Hasty said. People to hold things – horses, bits of clothing, that sort of thing. They want to borrow some horses, too—"

"They're not having Angus," eleven-year-old Dawn quickly interjected, her eyes wide with dismay, "I've seen what they do to horses in cowboy films."

"Really, Dawn! You *are* idiotic sometimes," Rachel sighed. "That's the old films. They're not allowed to be cruel nowadays."

Again, Jess jumped into the conversation, for she had seen the annoyance on Beckie's face when Rachel had spoken so disparagingly to Dawn. If only Beckie would realise that it was just Rachel's blunt way, and if only Rachel would think before she spoke . . .

"It's not a cowboy film, anyway, it's a smuggling film, set at the beginning of the last century. One of those costume dramas. They'll have another set, Mrs Hasty says, down at the estuary, by the old church."

The usually quiet Anna joined in with enthusiasm. "The perfect place for smuggling," she said excitedly. "All those steep, winding paths running down through the trees to the muddy estuary."

"*And* the church hill," Rachel put in. "It's

212

quite wild and windy there. There are caves in the rocks, too, below Church Walk."

"You see!" Jess looked round at them all. "It *is* going to be fun. We haven't sorted much out for the riding club – shall we go and look today?"

Even Beckie had to admit that the new arrivals in the golf club car park looked intriguing. Having ridden their ponies up the narrow private road towards the club, the eight Edgecombe Valley riders reined in their mounts and studied the scene.

Several large mobile-studio trailers were parked along one side of the car park. There were other vehicles, too; one or two motor bikes and a few large estate cars. Quite a large section of the car park seemed to have been taken over by a throng of noisy colourfully dressed people.

"Looks like a circus," Dawn murmured in a low voice to Jackie, who sat next to her astride her chestnut pony, Copper. Polly, in front of the two younger members of the club, snorted suspiciously, backing into Angus, Dawn's stocky skewbald, who moved obligingly.

"Let's investigate," suggested Sam, who was always eager to explore the unknown.

Brecon, her fourteen-hand bay pony, looked interested too, as he watched the comings and goings.

"I don't think we're allowed in the golf club," Anna said.

"Well, *they're* there," Rachel argued.

"Come on," said Richard, squeezing his big cob into life. "They can always turn us out if they want to. Let's have a look."

Richard, bareback astride Crusader, led the way through the entrance and into the car park. Two large, cobby horses, tethered under the hedge at the far side of the park, lifted their heads and whinnied.

A girl, hurrying across towards one of the mobile studios carrying a tray of drinks, grinned at them, and a man standing outside, dressed in a tattered shirt and knee-breeches, smiled too. His teeth showed white amid a dark bushy beard and moustache. His face was nut-brown and his hair long and untidy.

"*He's* brown," whispered Jackie to Dawn.

"It's make-up," Dawn replied.

As the eight rode up to the first trailer they were assailed by a voice. "Ah. Wonderful! Just what we want!"

The voice's owner materialised in the doorway of the large trailer van.

"Us, you mean?" Richard asked, disconcerted by the suddenness of the call.

The man stepped down from the van. He was short and tubby, untidily dressed in baggy brown trousers and a faded blue and white shirt. His hair was long and fine, and from under bushy eyebrows, bright blue eyes looked at them cheerfully. A wide, disarming smile spread across his pink and rather chubby face.

"Yes, you intrepid riders," he said, stopping at a safe distance from the ponies. "I'm a bit nervous of horses," he admitted, and then continued: "We were just talking about it, Ken and I. Not straight away, but perhaps in a few days. It'll be a night shoot."

Richard looked at the others and then back at Chubby Face. "Er . . . what exactly—"

"Graham's not always too clear."

Another man appeared at the top of the steps and then came down towards them. He was taller than his companion, and thinner, and walked with a slight limp. He, too, smiled at the riders; a slow, serious smile.

"We think we will need some extras, sometime next week," he explained. "Some riders and ponies. It will be for a night-time scene. Smugglers coming back from the coast; some

riding, some leading pack-horses, that sort of thing. And we could do with some horse help today, too. Interested?"

"Crusader enjoyed today's work!" Richard said with a grin, leaning backward on his pony's broad, bare back as a signal to halt. The bay cob stopped, settling himself comfortably in the shade.

"So did Brecon," Sam agreed, reining in her pony.

The other ponies, tired after their exertions, settled in the shade, standing around in various states of relaxation with heads hanging and legs resting, and tails swishing idly.

The "work" of the afternoon had consisted of cantering or trotting up and down the long, sloping field at the back of the golf club car park. The field led down towards the path at the edge of the channel, which lay still and bright as glass, with Wales beyond, misty in the heat. The work had been to make an authentic well-trodden bridle-path with the signs of use by many horses.

"I think the ponies are going to enjoy their film work," said ten-year-old Jackie Spalton, stroking Copper's chestnut neck.

"Polly loved it, too," Jess agreed. "It was fun."

"You *are* lucky, all of you," wailed Dawn. "I'm going on holiday next week. Angus and I will miss it all."

"Me too," sighed Anna.

"Never mind," Beckie comforted them, "you'll be back in time for the gymkhana."

"If it ever gets off the ground," Rachel broke in, her glance shifting towards Beckie.

Beckie swung round, her eyes flashing. "Of *course* it will," she replied sharply. "I told you we could have Justin's field by the motorway."

"But it's got to be *organised*," Rachel retorted. "Things don't just happen by themselves."

"Of course. I *know* that."

The girls glared at each other from their respective ponies.

"Oh, come on both of you," Jess interrupted. "It's too hot. We'll have a meeting about it. Next week. OK?"

The others murmured their agreement, and began to move off. No one liked it when Rachel and Beckie began to argue.

"See you Saturday, then," Richard called, as he prepared to turn his pony down towards Holder's Lane, which led to the valley. All but

Jess and Beckie, who was to stay the night at Jess's home, took the route down to Edgecombe Valley, from where they would make their various ways homeward.

Beckie was unusually quiet on the short journey home to Trumpeter Cottage. Glancing sideways at her friend, Jess wondered whether to say anything. She hated her two friends always being so much at loggerheads. But what could she say to improve the situation? Rachel was so outspoken and seemed never to think before she spoke. And Beckie, having only recently returned to the real world of walking and riding and being with other people, was extra sensitive. Jess frowned to herself as she tried to think it out. Rachel ought to be more understanding. But then again, Beckie needed to harden up a bit after her long hospital stay, and her time in the wheelchair . . .

"I think Polly might have a loose shoe." Beckie broke the silence, and the opportunity to talk about the problem was lost.

"Mm. You might be right," Jess agreed. "I thought I could hear a bit of a clink. Off hind?"

"Think so."

Chapter 3

"What do *you* think, Dad?"

It was the next evening and Jess, leaning against the warm stone of the stable wall, had explained to her father about the antagonism between Beckie and Rachel.

"It's spoiling the riding club," Jess added, with a sigh.

Mr Caswell paused in his digging, stopping to wipe his forehead and lean on the spade.

"I'm afraid, Jess," he said, looking across at his daughter, "there's not a lot you *can* do about it." As Jess looked questioning, he continued: "They'll either sort it out or they won't. I'm sorry," he added, "I know it doesn't seem much help, but it's true. You can't *make* two people like each other, just because they're your friends. Perhaps they'll always be sparking off against each other like this, and you'll just get used to it. Or maybe . . ." Dad picked up the spade again. "Maybe they'll learn to respect each other. Rachel's older than Beckie, isn't she – she's at that know-it-all stage. And

Beckie's had a bad time – probably feels a bit insecure."

"Mm. I suppose so . . ."

Dad set to work again. He was digging over a piece of the vegetable garden, and a pile of weeds and discarded vegetable stumps was growing on the path beside him.

"You just let it work itself out," Dad advised, adding another handful of weeds to the pile, "and fetch me the wheelbarrow, will you, if you're feeling helpful."

As Jess trundled the squeaky old wheelbarrow across the garden, a long and very arab snort came from the orchard. A grey head, held high, watched her suspiciously from over the hedge. Feigning fear, Polly was peering at Jess with wide eyes, her nostrils distended.

Jess lowered the wheelbarrow to the ground and went to speak to her pony. "You're just a great show-off," she told her, laughing. But remembering how ill the beautiful arab had been, earlier in the year, Jess delighted in watching the grey pony toss her head and trot off across the orchard with an exaggerated high-stepping action, snorting importantly.

Polly was not feeling quite so lively on the following Saturday, when a small contingent from the riding club met under the trees at the start of the golf club driveway. The air was heavy, and clouds of flies hung around the ponies. Heads shook and feet stamped. It was that clammy, sultry weather which causes friction amongst everyone – human or animal – and Jess was almost glad to see that Rachel was not there. In fact, only three others were waiting under the trees – Beckie on Justin, Richard bareback on Crusader, and Jackie mounted on Copper.

"Where is everyone?" Jess asked.

"Anna and Dawn have gone on holiday," Beckie explained.

"And we don't know where Sam or Rachel are," Richard added, "but we'd better get going, hadn't we?"

"We told them we'd be there by two o'clock," Jackie said. "Sticky, isn't it?" she added, as Jess and Polly came alongside her, and they all set off up the drive.

"Mm." Jess looked towards Castle Hill, where dark clouds rolled ominously behind the old ruined castle. "We *must* be going to have a storm sometime."

Ken, the director, and the assistant director, Graham, were also studying the stormy sky.

As the riders arrived at the car park, they could hear the two men discussing the weather.

"But it's obviously going to *pour* down, Ken. They'll get themselves ready and it'll just be an afternoon's filming wasted." Graham's pink chubby face looked troubled. "You know how difficult Sid can be when he gets ready and we don't film."

Ken nodded as Graham spoke. "I know, I know, but we ought to get on. The weather is so changeable anyway."

"But *really*," Graham flung an arm dramatically towards the darkened castle. "Be honest: it's going to rain, isn't it? And I *mean* rain!"

The director turned his gaze towards the four riders, who had halted their mounts close to the trailer van. All at once his normally serious face broke into a smile. "*I* know," he said, "we can do the scene where Fenella gallops through the storm—"

"But she's not here today. She's sick. We were hoping to do that scene next—"

"I know," Ken agreed, patting him on the shoulder reassuringly, "but we only need a hooded figure riding through a storm along the skyline for that scene – and then a loose horse galloping. Surely . . ." He turned his head in the direction of Richard and the three girls. "Surely we can persuade someone . . ."

Now Graham's face was wreathed in smiles, too. "Of course!" He looked towards them. "How about it, one of you girls? We need a lively horse—"

Richard, Beckie and Jackie all turned towards Jess and Polly.

"And the horse needs to come to the call, at a gallop," Ken added.

"We–ll," Jess admitted, when all eyes were upon her, "Polly *does* come when I call . . ."

"How about it, then?" Graham's round face looked at her, hopefully. "It'll save us a lot of trouble – and if it doesn't work out, there's no harm done."

Jess wasn't so sure. Helping out by galloping up and down a field was one thing, but actually being filmed . . .

"Go on, Jess, of course you can!"

Chapter 4

As Jess was helped into her cloak and long skirt, thunder rumbled around Castle Hill.

"I don't think Polly's going to like this," Jess murmured, half to herself. The woman from Wardrobe raised her eyebrows in sympathy and mumbled something through a mouthful of pins.

"There you are," she said, when all the pins had been removed from between her lips and were pinning up the hem of Jess's skirt and the end of the cloak sleeves. "That's fine, now. Fenella's quite small, so it didn't need much altering." She looked across at Jess. "Did your mum and dad give permission?" she asked.

Jess nodded. "Your director spoke to Mum on the telephone."

"Ken, you mean? That's all right, then." The woman cast a look in the direction of the van door, which was ajar. The first drops of rain were falling. "You're going to get soaked, I'm afraid," she told Jess.

"That's the idea, I think," Jess replied.

"Never mind. You can have a nice shower afterwards."

Out in the rain, as Jess was given a leg-up on to a somewhat jumpy Polly, she heard Ken's voice.

"Quiet for rehearsal, please." He hurried over to Jess and peered up at her from the depths of his waterproof clothing. Polly jumped sideways, frightened by the rustling anorak. Ken stepped back, eyeing Polly warily.

"Sorry, horse," he murmured. Then to Jess he added, "Now you know what to do, don't you? Hopefully, we'll only need one rehearsal. In fact . . ." He hesitated and then continued. "Perhaps we'll go straight in to shoot. We'll give it a try."

"OK, everyone!" Ken called out. "Change of plan. We'll shoot straight away. Grips! I'd like to do a short track on this. Make it quick. We don't know how long this weather will last!"

As Jess walked Polly round the car park to keep her warm, instructions were called out and figures hurried to and from one of the estate cars.

"Get me two sets of track and set up a Panther!" called a voice.

"Get me a five-K and stand," called another.

Large umbrellas appeared, held over the camera and lighting.

"Let's have some wild track while we're waiting," the soundman called.

"What *are* they all talking about?" Jess murmured to Polly, leaning forward to pat the pony's neck, which was already dark with rain. Polly flicked back an ear and snorted, shaking the rain from her long mane.

At last all seemed to be ready, and Jess was signalled at to move to the field, where camera and lighting were waiting.

"Quiet, please! First positions!"

Jess trembled with excitement and she felt Polly quivering too, as she saw the camera and lights.

"Running up!" came a voice from beneath an umbrella, held over the large camera where the cameraman sat. "Camera running!"

"Sound ready!" came another voice.

A bell rang, and Ken called, "Mark it!"

A figure in oilskins moved forward in the rain, holding the clapperboard in front of the camera. "One-eight-six," he called, "take one!" He snapped down the board with a sharp crack and as he did, and Ken the director called "Action!" Polly shot away, alarmed by the noise.

Almost unseated by Polly's instant obedience to Ken's command, Jess clung to the mane for a second and then righted herself, leaning forward into the rain and wind. Her cloak flowed out behind her, and the sound of Polly's thundering hooves pounded in her head.

Released from the frightening noise and clamour, Polly galloped down the field and Jess was hardly aware of any cameras or people. She knew that she must steer her pony on a course which ended at the bottom of the field where, earlier that week, she and Polly had helped to produce the well-worn path.

As they reached the path and she pulled up her pony, Jess gaped in astonishment. She blinked, wondering if her imagination were playing tricks on her, and rain trickled through her lashes into her eyes. But it was still there. Where before there had been just the edge of the field, and the bramble hedge which produced a plentiful crop of blackberries in August and September, there was now a weather-beaten old cottage, nestled into the hillside, looking as if it had been there for a hundred years or more!

"Goodness!" said Jess to Polly. "Wherever did *that* come from?" She squeezed her pony's sides, and Polly moved forward cautiously.

It was unbelievable. An old, stone, moss-covered cottage with a thick, weather-beaten pine door stood before them. The roof looked weatherproof, but in places one or two tiles had slipped a little, and the whole surface seemed to be covered with greeny-grey lichen. Suddenly panic-stricken, Jess looked about her. She must have galloped Polly the wrong way – missed the proper path. She'd spoiled the filming!

Several figures appeared over the brow of the hill, battling their way through the wind and rain of the storm.

"Wonderful!" called Ken from beneath his anorak hood. Richard, hurrying beside him dressed in borrowed oilskins, grinned at Jess. "You look wet!" he commented, unnecessarily.

Jess pulled a face at Richard and then turned to Ken. "But . . . I'm in the wrong place –" she said, her voice puzzled, "aren't I?"

It was Ken's turn to look puzzled. "No, that was good, Jess. There's the path you all made, last week. You were Tamzin Fry, galloping down to Jim's cottage to warn him—"

"Jim's cottage?" Jess echoed.

Beneath the hood, Ken's face broke into a smile. "Oh, the cottage. Of course. I see. It wasn't there before, was it?" He waved a hand in the direction of the old "stone" building. "It's all fibreglass," he explained. "They put it up in two days. Good, isn't it?"

Before Jess had any time to comment, Ken continued briskly. "We must do the second part before the storm finishes. This has all been very useful, Jess. I hope your horse will perform, now."

"I came to hold her," Richard explained. "I thought she might prefer someone she knows."

"Thanks. I'm glad you thought of that," Jess replied, imagining Polly's reaction to being grasped somewhat gingerly by an oilskin-clad stranger, perhaps even carrying an umbrella! As it was, Richard had a job to hold her as the camera and sound crew arrived, rattling and bumping their equipment, which was being carefully protected from the storm by large, brightly-coloured golf umbrellas.

"Now then," Ken explained, "Graham is back there. If you just go back to where you started, as quickly as you can, I'll be in contact with him as soon as we're ready." Ken tapped his radio which was attached to a belt underneath his waterproofs. "He'll tell you when to call your horse."

"I can't be too far away. She must be able to hear me," Jess pointed out.

"Well, stop when you think you're far enough away, and then when you've called her and she's started off, you run back. That way we should get enough film."

If it works, Jess thought, as she hurried away up the hill, having given Polly a quick hug and a lump of sugar. Sugar lumps, produced by Richard, had been a good idea. If Polly thought that there was something to eat at the end of it, she'd gallop over half of England!

"I gather it went well." Graham's round, cheerful face appeared in Jess's line of vision underneath the inevitable umbrella. "D'you want to come under?"

"It's OK, thanks," Jess replied with a grin. "I think I'm too wet to care, now!" She turned back. Polly and Richard were still in sight, a little way from the film crew. "I think she'll be able to hear me from here."

Graham pulled out his radio and spoke into it. "We're in position, Ken. Ready to roll?" He listened and then spoke to Jess. "A few minutes," he said. "When I get the OK from

Ken, I'll lower my arm and then get out of your way." He looked anxiously into the distance, in Polly's direction, before listening again to the radio with his arm raised.

Jess moistened her lips, nervously preparing them for the all-important whistle. They'd better hurry, she thought, eyeing the sky. There was a slightly paler grey break in the clouds just above the castle . . .

Graham's arm came down, and he turned and ran back towards the car park. Taking a deep breath and moistening her lips again, Jess whistled her special pony whistle – the one to which Polly and Muffin always came at a canter. Nothing seemed to happen so Jess whistled again, long and clear.

Then she saw Polly leap away from Richard. She was galloping towards Jess, stirrup irons banging against the saddle, reins flapping, her mane and tail streaming in the wind. Relief flooded through Jess – so much so that she almost forgot that she too had to run, so that Polly's wild gallop would be recorded for enough time on the film. Picking up her wet skirts Jess turned and ran for the golf club car park, the rain beating into her face and wet grass slapping at her legs.

Chapter 5

Jess had nearly reached the car park by the time a slightly puzzled Polly came trotting up behind her, breathing heavily and champing impatiently as if to say, "You called me and I came, and now you're running away from me. What's going on!"

Stopping, Jess turned and put her arms around her pony.

"You're a very good, clever girl," she told her, finding another lump of sugar and offering it. The reward was gratefully received, and a grey nose pushed its way into the folds of Jess's cloak. "It's no good," she laughed, "there's no more."

Graham appeared cautiously from behind the car park wall. Seeing Polly being firmly grasped by Jess, he stepped out. "It went well," he told her. "Ken's very pleased."

Graham looked at Jess, who stood dripping from any part of her or her clothing that was able to drip. Now that the excitement was over she had begun to shiver, and Polly too was beginning to tremble with cold rather than excitement. "I think you ought to change into some dry clothes," the assistant director said firmly, "or we'll be in trouble with your mum."

"I *am* cold now," Jess admitted, her teeth chattering, "but I must get home and dry Polly. I don't want her catching a chill. She was very ill earlier this year."

Graham turned and walked beside her as she made her way into the car park. "Now don't you worry about the horse," he said. "We've got a lad who's very good with horses. One of the Sparks's assistants, he is. The other ponies are all in the dry. I'll get young Kevin to see to her, and you must go off to Wardrobe for a shower and some dry clothes."

"Well, I'm not sure . . ."

"There he is. Kevin! Over here, a minute!"

Kevin hurried over, and Graham explained. Kevin's eyes lit up with interest. "Great," he said, "it'll make a change from lighting! Don't you worry," he added, turning to Jess, "I'll get a couple of others and we'll rub her down with straw until she's warmed up and dry, and then I'll put a rug on her. We've got some for the hire horses, and we've got a makeshift stable." He grinned. "It looks a bit peculiar, because it's really a tent, but it's weatherproof."

Jess was still doubtful, but now she was shivering uncontrollably. The storm had brought with it a chill wind. "She's a bit of a handful," Jess advised Kevin, but Polly, quiet as a lamb, allowed herself to be led away by a delighted assistant electrician, so Jess also allowed herself to be led away. A hot shower and dry clothes seemed the best things in life just now!

When Jess emerged from the wardrobe van twenty minutes later, the car park seemed to be deserted. The rain had just about stopped, and the grey of the sky was turning paler by the minute.

"Hi!" came a call from the director's van, and Ken appeared at the top of the steps, a mug in his hand. "Feeling better now?" Not waiting for a reply, he added, "Your friends are over there in Arthur's caravan. Goodness knows how they managed it. He's usually such a loner, these days." Ken descended the steps and came closer to Jess as he continued in a confidential tone. "His wife died two years ago. He just hasn't been the same since. He has ... problems." He waved an arm in the direction of the caravan. "Go and join them. Give Arthur a bit more company. It'll do him good. He's a good actor, but sometimes he gets . . . difficult, you see. Perhaps you youngsters will be a help to him."

Not understanding at all what Ken was talking about, Jess made her way obediently to the caravan which stood in one corner of the car park. Tentatively, she knocked on the door and pushed it open.

"Good heavens! It's the ghost of Castle Hill!". It was Richard's voice that greeted her. He, Jackie and Beckie were all draped in various positions of comfort on the seats of the caravan. Jackie was stroking a small black and white Jack Russell, which was sitting on the seat beside her. With them was the man whom they had seen briefly on their first visit to the film set – the man with the bushy beard and brown face who had smiled at them; but now he was clean-shaven and paler.

Jess giggled, realising that she was dressed all in white – white jogging-suit top with a hood which she had pulled up against the drizzle and white, loose trousers, several sizes too big for her. It was the best that Marjorie, the wardrobe mistress, had been able to find to replace Jess's soaked clothes.

"*Whoo-oo-oo,*" Jess wailed, raising her arms above her head in true ghost-fashion. "What a

lovely caravan," she added, pulling down her hood and grinning at Arthur, "I hope you don't mind, but Ken said the others were here."

"Of course not," Arthur assured her. "It's good to have company. Would you like some hot chocolate, too? We all got a bit cold in that heavy rain. You wouldn't think it could go so cold, would you – it was so sticky earlier."

Jess settled down with the others, and sipped at her hot drink as Arthur chattered. She wondered what Ken had been talking about. Arthur seemed friendly and cheerful, and his caravan was cosy and comfortable.

"Do the other actors live in caravans?" Jackie asked.

"No. They mostly stay at hotels," Arthur explained. "Me – I like to be independent. Do for myself. I'm not . . . not a good mixer, I'm afraid." He patted his dog, which had deserted Jackie and was sitting at his feet. "As long as I've got old Jock here, I'm all right," he added.

Arthur soon had them all laughing as he told them stories of acting life, and of the antics of some of the directors and technicians. Jess noticed that he didn't mention his own life, unless it was as a part of some funny happening on the set.

Arthur's entertainment was interrupted by a knock on the door. The door opened and Graham's head appeared.

"Tea break over, Arthur," he said. "Your scene next. You're wanted in Wardrobe and Make-up."

Out in the car park all was bustle again. Arthur and two other actors hurried over for attention from Make-up and Wardrobe, and Ken, Graham and a cameraman stood in a huddle beside one of the vans, deep in conversation. Guiltily Jess remembered Polly, realising that she had forgotten all about her while she had been listening to Arthur's stories.

She hurried over to the stable tent where Kevin was standing beside the grey arab, talking to her. Polly, clothed in a rug which was much too big for her, looked warm and comfortable.

"I'll have to go now," Kevin admitted. "I'm glad you came." He patted Polly's neck. "She's a lovely pony," he said. "I used to have one when I was a kid – about the same height but heavier; more of a cob."

"Thanks for looking after her," Jess called, as Kevin hurried away.

Jackie appeared beside Jess. "We thought we might go home now," she told Jess. "Beckie thinks there might be another storm, and my mum's expecting me back for tea."

"I'd better get back too. I'd like to have watched Arthur's scene, though."

"Apparently it's only a tiny one," Jackie told her. "It just shows Arthur outside his cottage—"

"Oh – he's Jim, is he?"

"Yes, that's it. He just has to study the skyline and look worried, and then hurry off in the direction of the cove."

"What cove?" Jess asked, looking puzzled. There was no cove below Jim's cottage.

Jackie laughed. "Silly, isn't it?' she said. "The cove is meant to be below the cottage, but they shoot it at the estuary, by the old church. They're going there tomorrow for one of Arthur's cove scenes."

"What about Tamzin?" Jess asked, as she pulled off Polly's oversized rug and began to saddle up her pony. "What happens to her? You seem to know the story."

"She ends up lying face down in the mud, with blood dripping from her forehead after she falls off," Jackie told her cheerfully, as she tightened the girth on Copper's saddle, "but that'll be taken next week when Fenella's back."

"I'm glad I don't have to do that, too," Jess laughed. "It's a complicated business, this film-making," she added. "How do you know what happens?"

"Arthur's been telling us about it," Beckie explained. She and Richard had arrived, and now began saddling up their ponies. "He's really nice."

As Jess hurried over to the wardrobe van to collect her wet clothes, which Marjorie had put into two plastic bags, she wondered what Arthur's "problem" was. Just loneliness, she supposed, since the death of his wife.

As they all set off on their ponies, Jess with the two plastic bags slung over the pommel of her saddle, Ken called out to them. "We'll be down at the estuary next Tuesday," he said, "for the night shoot. Are you all on for being smugglers?"

Chapter 6

"What happened to you and Sam?"

"Oh, well, we were late anyway, and then Bee lost a shoe. Brecon was acting up, too – Sam says he gets like that sometimes, when there's a storm coming. And it was obviously going to *tip* down, so we turned back. What happened? Was it called off?"

"No," Jess replied a little smugly to Rachel, down the telephone. "Polly was acting up, too! Polly and I were filmed!"

For once Rachel was speechless. She was suitably impressed when Jess explained. "You wait till I tell Sam what we missed," she said, adding: "Will there be any more acting?"

"There's the smuggling scene – next Tuesday. They're filming all afternoon and into the night."

"Of course! I'd forgotten. Great! How are we going to get home?"

Now it was Jess's turn to be silent for a moment. "I hadn't thought of that," she admitted. "Horseboxes, maybe. We'll talk about it tomorrow."

"Oh yes, the gymkhana meeting." Rachel's voice sounded less enthusiastic. "Beckie's field . . . I only hope—"

"Rachel, I—"

"Sorry Jess, got to go. Forgot I promised to take Sach for his walk. He's going bananas! Rushing around the hall like a lunatic, with his lead in his mouth!"

"See you tomorrow, then. My house." Jess sighed as she replaced the receiver. "Dandy," she said to her young cat, bending down to stroke him as he wove his way around her legs, purring loudly. "I just hope they don't argue too much tomorrow."

The Edgecombe Valley Riding Club meetings were always informal affairs. They were held in a shed next to the stable at Trumpeter Cottage. There were bales of straw and hay to sit on, the roof didn't leak and, for gloomier days, there was electric lighting. "All mod cons," as Sam put it. Everyone agreed that they felt more *ponyish* somehow, sitting amongst saddles and bridles, with the smell of hay and saddle soap pervading the air. Doubtless, too, Mrs Caswell's tray of lemonade and home-made chocolate cake, brought in part-way through the proceedings by Tommy, added extra appeal to the venue.

The Monday afternoon meeting began amicably enough. The five others arrived at Jess's home more or less on time. All came on their bicycles except Richard, who arrived on foot, accompanied by Columbus.

"We're all resting our smuggling ponies, are we?" asked Jess with a grin.

"I can't get the blacksmith until tomorrow morning," Rachel explained, draping herself over one of the hay bales.

"I had to go shopping with Mum this morning," Sam said, "and I didn't have time to get Brecon ready." She wrinkled her nose in disgust. "I need a new carpet in my bedroom, apparently, and Mum said I had to choose the colour!" She sighed. "I'd much rather have had a new saddle, but there you are, that's parents for you!"

Jess, the unofficial chairman of the meetings, said, "Shall we begin, then?"

They discussed the following evening, and it was decided that Rachel and Beckie should ask their respective parents if they would collect them, with horseboxes. Somehow, Sam's earlier comment about parents had been forgotten!

"But that's only four," Jackie pointed out. "Two in Beckie's box and two in Rachel's. What about the other two?"

Richard, stretched out under the window with his legs along a bale of straw and his head resting in the cobwebs, said, "I think I might ride home. With a lantern or torch. I like being out at night – you sometimes see foxes, or even a badger."

"Hey!" Sam leaned forward, her eyes shining with interest. "That sounds great! I'd like to do that . . . but I don't know if my parents would let me.'

"Well, your house is on the way home for me. Surely if there are two of us . . ."

". . . And they *could* always drive to meet me if they're worried . . ."

"Well, let's hope it all works out," said Jess, anxious to get on with the meeting. "Shall we discuss the gymkhana now?"

Everyone shifted uneasily on their straw bales, and a slight feeling of tension crept into the small shed. Rachel leaned forward and looked in Beckie's direction. "The first thing is, have we got a field?" she asked. "We can't have a gymkhana without a field."

Beckie sighed. "You *know* we can have Justin's field by the motorway," she said. "I told you last week—"

"But have you checked it with the farmer? He might not like a gymkhana in his field. It might get churned up if the weather's wet. Had you thought of that?"

"Well . . . no . . . but—"

"Well, how can we have a meeting about a gymkhana until we *know* we have a field to hold it in?"

Beckie glared across the shed at Rachel. "Well, I'm sure Mr Ford won't mind," she said, "but I haven't actually asked him yet."

"That's pretty hopeless, isn't it?" Rachel said, exasperated.

Beckie flushed angrily. "Well, I—"

"Look," Jess interrupted quickly, "Why don't we discuss the gymkhana, assuming that it's all right to have Mr Ford's field, and then Beckie can ask him."

"But I—" began Rachel, but she too was interrupted, this time by Richard.

"That's the best idea," he said, pulling a piece of paper from his pocket. "I've made a list of events I could think of." Without waiting for approval, he began to read out the list, and Jess looked across at him gratefully. For a moment, Beckie and Rachel had looked as if they were about to stand up and begin shouting at each other!

Somehow Jess and Richard, with some help from Sam with Jackie, managed to steer the rest of the meeting through various discussions without Rachel and Beckie actually coming to blows, but Jess was glad when the last bicycle had disappeared round the bend in the lane.

"How was the meeting?" Mum asked, seeing Jess on the path.

"*Just* about peaceful!"

"Rachel and Beckie?"

Jess nodded.

"What a shame," said Mrs Caswell. "I hope it doesn't spoil the club."

The same thought was running through Jess's mind as she wheeled her bicycle from the garage and out of the gate. She paused. While the meeting had been in progress, a wind had been getting up, rattling the wooden door of the shed and blowing branches against the window so that long, leafy fingers had scratched at the glass. Now a gale was blowing, and dark clouds were advancing from the south-west, threatening a storm.

Jess zipped up her anorak and set off. She

go to check about times for tomorrow. Otherwise, she thought, looking up at the dark sky and feeling the buffeting wind, she would stay at home. It wasn't far to the golf club, so maybe she would get there and back before the rain arrived.

It was hard work battling against the wind, and the strength of the gale seemed to be increasing. At the top of Holder's Lane, where there was no protection from trees or houses, the wind almost knocked Jess sideways. Hastily, she dismounted and pushed her bike, feeling safer walking but wishing that she hadn't set out. Still, the golf club was closer than home, so she put her head down and pushed her way through the gale.

As Jess climbed the hill towards the golf club the wind grew even stronger, and she felt the breath being blown out of her body. Passing Castle Cottage, halfway up the hill, Jess saw that some tiles had blown off the roof. Old Mr Simpson was in his garden, gazing up with dismay at the hole in his roof, his white hair blowing forward over his face. He and Jess waved and shouted at each other about the storm, but the wind snatched their words and tossed them away, unheard.

Jess battled on, passing the old ruined castle,

and made her way to the golf club ca
As she entered, the car park appeared emp
Neither Ken nor Graham were there, enscon-
sed in their van drinking coffee and discussing
the filming, as usual. The wardrobe van was
empty, too.

Having left her bicycle propped against a
wall, Jess wandered around the set feeling
more and more puzzled. Surely they wouldn't
all have gone... As she reached the rise of
the hill, at last Jess saw them. They were all
gathered around Arthur's caravan – or what
was left of it!

Putting her head down again Jess battled
against the wind, which now seemed even
stronger. It was roaring through the trees and
screaming across the tarmacked ground, picking up anything it could find. Old plastic bags,
sticks and crisp-packets had been snatched
from their hiding-places and were swirling
around in a crazy storm dance.

As Jess approached she could see that the
caravan had been partially crushed by a large
elm tree, which had fallen across the front.
Everyone had gathered around the caravan,
and Arthur was sitting on the ground next to
it, looking dazed and confused.

"Hello, Jess!" Marjorie, the wardrobe mis-

Chapter 7

Graham explained as he and Jess fought their way back towards the mobile studio.

"It's since his wife died," he told her. "If anything goes wrong, then he goes on the bottle. It's nearly lost him his job twice, but we keep sorting him out. He promised after the last time," Graham added, "that he wouldn't touch drink again. Said he'd learned his lesson—"

"What happened, then?" asked Jess.

"It's his dog," Graham told her as they reached the van, "Little Jock – he's gone missing."

"Oh, poor Arthur." They had reached the relative quiet of the van and Jess was able to speak in a normal voice. "When did he first miss him?"

"Last night. Jock had his supper with Arthur as usual and then Arthur let him out – and he hasn't come back. As a matter of fact," Graham added slowly, "we were just wondering when you came . . ."

Jess looked across at the assistant director curiously.

"Arthur's caravan's a wreck," Graham continued. "We might be able to sort out a make-shift place for him in one of the vans but . . . well, we'll just have this trouble again, if we leave him."

"You mean the drinking?"

"That's it. Last night, when he'd called and searched and couldn't find Jock – he just legged it to the pub. Goodness knows how he got back. We didn't know where he'd gone, and then this morning we found him in his van, rolling drunk. He'd brought some bottles back with him, you see."

"And now his van's a mess."

Graham sat down, looking worried. "And we're in a mess, too, if we can't keep him sober. And *that* takes pots of coffee and hours of patience, each time."

"So how can I help?" asked Jess.

Graham looked at her hopefully. "Well, we were wondering," he explained, "if you knew of somewhere he could stay – where someone could keep an eye on him." As Jess looked surprised, Graham continued to explain. "The others are in a hotel in Catley," he said, "but that's no good for Arthur. I can't expect the others to watch him all the time. Everyone *likes* him, but he's such a loner. No one knows him very well. We thought," Graham continued, leaning forward, "that you might know of a place in your village that does bed and breakfast – somewhere small. You know what I mean?"

Jess was quiet for a moment, her mind wandering about the village of Edgecombe. Somewhere small, where Arthur would be looked after well, and made to feel at home . . .

"I think I know," Jess cried at last, "if she'll do it. The perfect place! Mrs Hasty at the post office!"

"He's such a *nice* man, Mrs Hasty, but he's lonely, you see. Since his wife died. And now he's lost his dog." Jess found herself gabbling incoherently across the post office counter. Having been blown down the lane from the castle into the village of Edgecombe, Jess had arrived breathless at the post office door, just as Mrs Hasty had been about to close for the night.

Mrs Hasty lifted the counter flap and came into the shop.

"Now look, my dear," she said, as she locked the post office door securely from the inside, "that old storm has knocked all the air out of you. You come on into my back room and we'll put the kettle on. I've been on my feet all day, and I could do with a cup of tea. And I made one of my cherry and almond cakes yesterday ..."

Sitting in Mrs Hasty's cosy back room away from the roar of the storm, Jess knew that she had chosen well for Arthur.

"Of course I can put him up, my dear," Mrs Hasty told her in her warm, untroubled voice as she moved the plate of cherry cake in Jess's direction. "And," she leaned forward conspiratorially, "I'll keep a good eye on him. I had an aunt, you know, who married a chap who liked his drink a bit too much, and d'you know what she did with him?"

Jess shook her head, unable to speak through the cake.

Mrs Hasty chuckled. "They had a village store, you know, like this one," she told Jess, "and she kept him so busy that he didn't have *time* for the drink and then he just ... lost the habit!"

Jess had surfaced from the delicious depths of the cherry cake and was now able to speak. "Perhaps you'll do the same with Arthur, Mrs Hasty," she said.

Mrs Hasty began chuckling again, but this time louder. "What dear, keep him too busy, or marry him?"

Chapter 8

The storm blew itself out during the night, and in the morning, the sky was clear and the countryside calm and still.

Having telephoned early to the other members of the riding club, Jess's first visit of the day on her bicycle was to Edgecombe post office, where she was surprised to find Arthur serving behind the counter of the store.

"I thought you were filming today," Jess said.

"I *am*," Arthur confirmed, "but your friend there," he jerked his head in the direction of the post office grille, behind which Mrs Hasty was busy dispensing stamps, postal orders and child benefit, "she's a regular slave-driver! Had me up this morning at half past six. Half past six!" he repeated. "D'you know," he said, "I didn't know a time like that *existed*! She made me a wonderful breakfast, though," he added. "Egg, bacon, sausage, the lot. And then she made me wash up!"

Jess caught a glimpse of Mrs Hasty behind

the post office counter, and received a knowing wink from her.

"What about your filming?" Jess persisted.

"Ken said we'd start an hour late, at ten o'clock," Arthur explained. "He guessed I'd like a lie-in, after yesterday's happenings!" Arthur chuckled again at the thought of his lie-in, and Jess noticed how happy he looked.

"We're all going out to search for Jock this morning," she promised him, "I'm sure we'll find him for you."

It wouldn't be easy, though, Jess reminded herself as she put a foot into the stirrup and swung herself up into Polly's saddle. The grey mare danced and jigged on the spot, chewing on her snaffle-bit and looking about her expectantly. Where do you start looking for a small black and white terrier, Jess wondered, as she squeezed Polly's sides with her heels, causing the pony to move off swiftly. Arthur had told her that Jack loved digging in rabbit holes. Perhaps he was stuck somewhere in one of the hundreds of rabbit warrens around the old castle, and along the edges of the golf-course? Or maybe he had wandered further, into another village, and someone had thought he was a stray.

Jess's musings took her and Polly to the top of Holder's Lane, where she met Richard and Sam as planned. Beckie and Jackie arrived a few minutes later.

"I've been to the police station to report Jock missing," Jess told the others, "and Mrs Hasty will tell everyone else. What she doesn't know about what happens in the village doesn't bear telling!"

"We'd better split up, hadn't we," Richard suggested, "and meet back here in ... two hours?"

"You go in twos," Jess proposed, "and I'll go on my own. I know the area better than any of you. Beckie, you and Jackie could try along the coast path, where Jim's cottage is, and Richard and Sam, you could go round the other side of the golf-course. I'll go through the woods and look for him there." She frowned. "If he's on the golf-course itself we can't do much about it. I don't think the golfers would appreciate the ponies cantering across their greens! Besides, surely they'd see Jock. There's enough of them, after all."

"And Arthur went into the golf club to tell them, before he got drunk," said Jackie, "Graham told me."

"Right!" said Sam, determinedly, pressing

her heels into Brecon's sides, "Edgecombe Valley Riding Club rescue section is under way!"

They separated at the top of the narrow private lane which led to the golf-course. Jess turned right towards the castle and the woods below, which ran along the west side of the Edgecombe valley. Richard and Sam continued straight ahead towards the common, and Beckie and Jackie trotted towards the golf club car park, from where they would ride down over the fields to the wide coastal path.

Jess cantered Polly over the short springy turf of Castle Hill towards the old castle itself. She knew that Arthur had searched there but it seemed sensible to check again. Polly jogged suspiciously among the ruins as Jess's eyes searched the overgrown stones for any signs of a small Jack Russell with a black smudge above his left eye and bright, inquisitive eyes.

"Nothing here, Polly," Jess murmured at last, guiding her pony out through the entrance to the keep, and down a narrow rabbit path towards the woods.

Sunlight was intermittent in the woods. In some places it dappled the undergrowth and the leafy path, and sometimes it was almost obscured by the density of the foliage. In these places the wood was dark and gloomy, and the rustlings of birds and small animals made both Polly and Jess start. But all the rustles were false alarms. There was no sign of Jock, and at last Jess and her pony arrived at the lane which led through Edgecombe Valley to Porterbury.

There was still plenty of time to spare, so Jess rode Polly along the lane for about half a mile and then re-entered the wood, nearer to the common. Again they wandered through the dark and sometimes gloomy wood, with Jess calling every now and then: "Jock! Where are you? Good boy, come on, Jock!" But the only replies she received were the startled cry of a blackbird, disturbed from its scratching for food among the leaves, and the scolding chatter of a squirrel which ran across a branch in front of her and leapt across to the next tree.

As she rode through the wood, Jess found herself wondering about the other problem – Beckie and Rachel. Rachel had not been able to come this morning, since Beetle was being shod, and so there had been no arguments. But later on that day, when they would all be at the estuary for the smuggling scenes, would the two of them quarrel, Jess wondered?

"Stop worrying about it," Sam advised, when Jess confided her fears as they rode together back to Trumpeter Cottage, after the fruitless search. Beckie, riding Justin, was a little way ahead with Richard and Jackie, and was out of earshot. "Let them sort it out," Sam added, leaning forward to flick a horsefly from Brecon's sturdy neck, "I think the riding club's great – the best thing that's happened to me since I got Brecon. It's just a nuisance when they argue so much, that's all."

Jess, who worried and thought things over so much, envied Sam her casual matter-of-fact approach and vowed to be more like her.

Rachel and Beetle joined them at Trumpeter Cottage and, after a picnic lunch in the orchard, they all set off again, this time in the direction of the estuary, a journey of about a mile through country lanes towards the channel.

Clereton Estuary was an attractive setting; wide and muddy where the river Clere meandered its way through mud-flats to the channel. A few boats rested on the shore or lay at odd angles on the banks of the river, stranded by the outgoing tide but secured to their moorings. Overlooking the flat, watery scene was the old church, tucked in under

Church Hill, but well above water-level. Church Hill was a wild and often windy place, with a winding path running round its edge above cliffs, at the bottom of which were huge, seaweed-covered rocks where the waves lapped, or sometimes crashed, against them.

"Beautiful, isn't it?" Beckie breathed, when they arrived at the gate which led into the estuary field.

Rachel, struggling to lift the latch on the gate, began to mutter about the practicalities of life, but Jess interrupted quickly. "Oh, look, there's Arthur. I hope he's sober!"

"I should think so," Richard said with a grin, "he seems to have his bodyguard with him!"

"So he has," said Jess, gazing in astonishment at Mrs Hasty, dressed in her Sunday best and comfortably settled on a canvas chair, next to the generator van known affectionately by the crew as "Genny". "She must have found someone to help at the shop. Tuesday's one of her busy days – she told me. She's really taking her Arthur-duties seriously!"

The filming was under way. Arthur, dressed in his old shirt and knee-breeches and wearing the false beard and moustache, was scuttling down the path towards the water's edge, peering nervously behind him from time to time, closely followed by the camera crew. From behind one of the rocks, there appeared a shifty-looking character wearing clothes even more tattered than Arthur's and darting furtive glances over his shoulder, as the two of them talked together.

"What's that fluffy thing they're hanging over Arthur's head?" Jackie hissed in Jess's ear.

"It's called a boom," Jess whispered back. They had all learned by now that silence was required while filming was taking place. "Kevin told me about it. It's recording the sound – their conversation and the sound of the water."

"Cut!" called Ken, and everyone relaxed and began talking again. Graham hurried over to meet them, as the riders approached. "We shan't be shooting your scene for a long time," he told them.

"It's OK, we know," Richard explained, "we came to watch Arthur's scene."

The filming continued into the early evening, and then Graham called a halt for supper. Whatever else went wrong, the film crew always managed to eat well. Their mobile café, which followed wherever the film crew went, had bumped its way down the stony path and now the actors were presented with a reasonably substantial meal, handed out from behind the hatch by two cooks.

"Come on, you intrepid riders," Graham urged. "You'll need something to keep you going into the night!"

With their ponies tied up along the fence, the six young prospective actors queued at the van and were given their meals. Arthur, just ahead of Jess in the queue, took two plates of food. He turned to Jess.

"Your Mrs Hasty is a fine woman," he told her.

"How did she manage to get away from the shop?" Jess asked.

"Got her niece in from over the road," Arthur explained.

Jess and the others joined Arthur and Mrs Hasty. They were sitting near the pebbly little beach which was tucked in between the estuary and the granite rocks which lay beneath the cliff-edge of Church Hill. Perching themselves on some of the rocks, the six friends devoured their meal in appreciative silence, while the sun sank dramatically over the horizon turning the sea, river, mud and rocks to pink and gold.

"You know," said Mrs Hasty, leaning back in her canvas chair and watching pink and gold seagulls strutting across the mud, "I never knew how beautiful it could be down here – and I've lived in these parts for longer than I care to think."

"It's certainly a gorgeous night," Jess agreed.

"Lovely, isn't it," added Arthur.

The director disturbed their reverie. "Let's clear away and make a start," he called, standing above them in the dusk. "By the time we've sorted ourselves out, the moon will be up and we can begin the night-time smuggling shoot. Are you paying attention, smugglers?"

The Edgecombe Valley Riding Club members turned to listen.

"You all go to see Marjorie in Wardrobe, and then Kevin will help you with your ponies," said Ken. "OK, Pete?" he added. "You can manage without young Kev tonight, can't you?"

"Even better than with him!" came the joking reply from somewhere in the ever-deepening dusk.

"We'd better have some more lighting, Sparks," Ken added, "And Arthur, you and Sid come and see me, please."

All at once, the rocky track and grassy area was a hive of industry with people hurrying about, cameras and lights being wheeled across and, every now and then, instructions being issued.

Kevin unsaddled the ponies and took them one by one over to Props, while the six riders made their way to the wardrobe van, where Marjorie dealt with them, quickly and efficiently. Three-quarters of an hour later, six dark-faced ruffians emerged to meet up with six ponies wearing bulging panniers and sacks on their backs.

"It's OK," said Kevin, seeing Jess's worried face as she looked at Polly's load, "it's mostly foam in there, with just some ballast to hold it down." He grinned, "Lighter than you, anyway," he added, wickedly.

"She seems to be taking it well," said Jess, "I thought she might object!"

Kevin laughed. "They all think there's food inside there," he told her. "I gave them pony-nuts while I filled the sacks, and I rustled about in the bags pretending the nuts came from there!"

They all gathered round Ken and Graham who gave them their instructions. "I think we can begin now," said Graham, looking up at the sky. "The moon's up and it'll be dark enough by the time we get into position."

There was a rehearsal first, and then the filming began. Each time, the ponies had to be led up the winding path to the top of Church Hill, and the cameras filmed their journey as they were led carefully down by their disguised owners. Every time, Ken was not quite satisfied.

"We must have walked *miles*," said Beckie, as the six prepared to lead their ponies up the hill for the fifth time.

Jess held her breath, waiting for Rachel to comment, but Beetle chose that moment to play up.

The ponies were beginning to tire of this new game, and everyone was pleased when, at the end of the next shot, Ken called out "Cut!" and then added, "That's it, all of you. That was a good one. Wrap it up!"

"What's he talking about?" asked Jackie.

"I presume that means we can go home," Richard murmured.

Jackie, stifling a yawn, said, "The horse-boxes have been here for ages. I saw them come just as we began the second take."

"I'm tired," Jess admitted, yawning. "And

so's Polly. I'm quite glad, now, that we're not riding home."

"Well, I'm looking forward to it," stated the ever-adventurous Sam. "I've got a torch, and lights to fit on my heels!'

It was when the horseboxes had left, by moonlight, and the film crew had dispersed that Sam, shining her torch to lead the way along the rough track from the estuary, quickly turned her head and reined in her pony.

"What's up?" asked Richard, halting Crusader.

"I – I thought I heard something."

"What sort of something?"

In the darkness Sam hesitated. Then she turned towards Richard. "I *thought*," she replied uncertainly, "that I heard a dog howling."

Chapter 9

"Sorry, Jess. I had to ring early. It's important."

"Sam! Aren't you tired after last night?"

"Well, yes, but – are you still there?"

A mumbled reply came from Jess, who had collapsed in a sleepy heap on the telephone table.

"Yes," came the yawning reply, "It's just so early and I'm tired—"

"Richie and I think we might know where Jock is—"

"What! Really?" Jess was suddenly awake. "Are you sure?"

"Well . . . no," Sam admitted, "but it's worth investigating."

"Where do you think he might be?"

"At the estuary." Sam explained about the howling. "We couldn't look *then* – it was too dark. But it's so quiet and lonely out there. Why would a dog be howling unless it was lost, or stuck? And he could be there somewhere, couldn't he? Arthur has taken him there a couple of times, when they were filming."

"We must go straight away, mustn't we?" Jess interrupted. "We *must* check. He's been lost for *days*!"

The telephone lines between Trumpeter Cottage and the homes of Beckie, Rachel and Jackie were soon humming as Jess explained and called a hasty meeting. "Don't bring the ponies," she instructed, "we may be scrambling about, and they might be a nuisance."

Jess was just puzzling out how to contact Richard when he arrived at the back door of the cottage, a rope slung over his shoulder and Columbus at his heels.

"I thought Col might sniff Jock out, if he *is* there somewhere," he told Jess, "he's pretty good like that."

When all six had gathered, they decided to travel to the estuary on foot. "It'll only take about twenty minutes," Jess said, "and besides, Richie hasn't got his bike. He came with Columbus."

So the six and Columbus set out on their rescue operation. The day was clear and fine and already, even though it was early, the sun was warm on their backs.

"What's in your rucksack, Jess?" Jackie asked.

"Money for the telephone and an old sheet," Jess replied. "And a rug. I thought if Jock's injured we might need to keep him warm," she explained, "and the sheet might be . . . useful."

"For tearing up for bandages – that sort of thing," said Jackie.

"Good idea," Beckie commented. "I hope it *is* Jock – and that he's all right."

They passed the church, grey, old and squat on its small hill, and continued down the long, winding lane which led to the estuary.

At the gate they paused, and Columbus ran along the river-bank, sniffing and investigating, disturbing a pair of moorhens which had been paddling about in the reeds. Beyond, the river wound like a silver snake towards the channel, and the morning sun glistened on the mud-flats.

"Quiet sort of place, isn't it," said Richard, "only the boats and the seagulls."

"And that fisherman," Rachel pointed out, nodding towards a distant figure on the mud-flats.

"He must have been up early," Sam commented.

"These fishing people will get up at *any* time to fish," said Beckie, "they're crazy!"

"Oh, I don't know—" Rachel began.

"Come on," Jess interrupted, "no time for fishermen. Where shall we start looking for Jock? Where did the howling come from, Sam?"

"Sort of that way," Sam replied, vaguely indicating the hill, "but I'm not sure exactly where."

"This way, then," said Jess, turning towards the well-known path up and down which they and the ponies had plodded so many times on the previous evening.

"Oh, no! Not again!"

This morning, however, the climb seemed easy without the ponies to lead, and with the hope of maybe finding Jock.

At the top they all paused to admire the view, but Jess soon urged them on.

"The hill's quite big," she said, "there are plenty of places he might be – stuck in a hole in the bramble bushes, or on that cliffy bit by the main beach, or the high cliffs above the rocks."

Jess was right. It was a large area to search. They spread out across the hill, walking slowly, calling to Jock. Columbus, not quite sure what it was all about but eager to help, ran backwards and forwards among them.

They scoured the hill, pushing their way through the long grass, following the narrow paths and struggling into thorny bramble hedges, in search of the little Jack Russell.

"I'm scratched to pieces," Sam stated, when they were all gathered together again above the steep, rocky incline which looked over a long, pebbly beach.

"Me too," Jackie agreed, looking at her bleeding, bramble-pricked hands. "P'raps you'll have to bandage *us* up with your sheet, Jess," she added, with a grin.

"I found plenty of holes," said Richard, "but no Jock. Where next?" he added.

"Down there, I suppose." Sam looked towards the steep, rocky edge between them and the beach. "Although I wouldn't have thought there would be many places there to get lost."

"There *are* some little caves among the rocks," Jess reminded her.

"Come on then," said Rachel, leading the way.

Taking different routes, they scrambled down the small clifflike incline. There were narrow paths among the rocks which made it more accessible. Between the rocks, as Jess had said, were small openings, but none contained Jock and no answer came to their calls.

"Jock gets to be quite a difficult word to keep repeating," Richard panted, as they reached the path at the bottom and met up again, "my throat's getting quite sore."

"He should have been called Laddie," Sam agreed, "much easier on the larynx!"

Sam was trying to be cheerful, but they were all starting to flag, and disappointment was setting in. Secretly, each one had hoped that Jock would soon be found. Now, one by one, they were beginning to think that they were on a wild-goose chase.

Jess produced a large bar of nut chocolate from her rucksack.

"Great!" said Sam, flopping down on the grass and leaning back against a rock, "Let's have a rest."

Agreement was unanimous. Jess divided the chocolate bar and they all munched in silence for a few minutes. Then, they all heard it, in the distance – a faint bark, followed by a howl.

"Which way was it?" demanded Jess, jumping up.

"Back the way we've come," said Richard, joining her.

"But further over – towards the channel," Rachel contributed.

"The cliffs!" they all chorused.

"Back, then – but along the cliff path, this time," said Jess excitedly. Hastily pushing the chocolate-bar paper back into her rucksack and swinging the bag over her shoulder, Jess hurried after the others who had already set off.

They ran and stopped to call and then ran again, along the narrow path enclosed on the cliff side by a wooden railing fence. And, gradually, the barking became less faint.

Rachel, in front, stopped on a slight rise at a place where the fence was broken. "It sounds about here," she panted, "but quite a way down the cliff."

"Of course, it might not be Jock," Beckie reminded them.

"Well, why does it keep barking when we call Jock?" Rachel snapped.

Sam broke in quickly. "We can't climb down . . . can we?" she asked, having peered gingerly over the edge. Below a sheer drop of about forty feet were the rocks – huge, grey, angry-looking boulders piled next to the cliff-face, the further ones lapped by the water of the channel.

"I did some rock-climbing at school camp," Richard observed doubtfully. "Perhaps—"

"I don't think the parents would think much of us clambering about down there," said Jess. Silent agreement filled the air as they all looked cautiously over the grassy edge to the menacing rocks far below.

"It doesn't look exactly . . . inviting, does it?" agreed Rachel, at last. As the eldest of the six would-be rescuers, she voiced all their thoughts.

"Why don't we," said Jess slowly, "go back to the beach and try walking along the rocks. See if we can see him. He sounds quite a way down."

This was agreed to be a brilliant suggestion, and they retraced their steps. At the beach, Jess stopped and turned to the others. She hesitated. "I've been thinking," she said at last, "he might be—"

"Yes, I have too," broke in Richard. "If he's fallen from right up there, he might be in a terrible state. Broken back . . . anything."

Jackie turned pale. "Poor little Jock," she breathed.

"Well, at least we've got the rug," said Sam briskly. "If he's as bad as that, we'll cover him up and go for help."

This agreed, Sam led the way over the rocks. Scrambling and sliding over the jagged and sometimes slimy rocks was difficult, and they all fell silent as they carefully negotiated footholds.

Columbus, slipping and sliding over the seaweed, thought it was a great pastime and he voiced his approval at regular intervals.

"I think we must be about there," Sam said at last, panting as she stood on a flat-topped rock.

"That's the place," Richard agreed, standing ankle-deep in seaweed. "I marked it in my mind by that little twisted tree up there." He pointed up to the cliff path, where some broken fence could just be seen next to the tree.

Everyone peered around. "Can't see Jock," said Jess, her voice flat with disappointment.

Then Columbus barked and jumped up on a rock which lay close to the cliff-face. He tried to clamber up, but his paws slipped on the rock. He barked again, wagging his tail, and a husky little bark came in return from above him.

"Where on earth—" Richard began.

"There he is!" Jackie said, pointing excitedly. "I can see a leg!"

They could all see it, now. It had looked like just another exposed root from one of several small, stunted bushes. Now that the children knew where to look they could see a tail, too, wagging furiously amid the roots and foliage, only about ten feet above them.

Richard let out a long, low whistle. "What a lucky little dog!" he exclaimed. "He must have been investigating at the top, gone through the broken fence and slipped."

"And he could have ended up down here, where we are," added Jess, "perhaps with broken bones, or even being killed!"

"But he was saved by that bush!" finished Rachel.

It took only a matter of minutes to release Jock from his bushy prison. Richard stood on the rock beneath the bush and Jackie, being the lightest, was lifted on to his shoulders.

"Don't look down," Richard advised, as Jackie wobbled precariously on his shoulders, afraid to straighten up, "and hang on to the roots. Then you'll be OK."

But when Jackie's head came level with Jock's wagging tail, she forgot her fears. Carefully, she reached up with her right hand whilst steadying herself with her left. She tucked her arm around Jock's thin body and

lifted him from the roots, which had trapped him and possibly saved his life. He yelped, and then proceeded to lick her face enthusiastically.

"I think he's hurt his leg," Jackie called down.

"Probably pulled something when he crashed into the bush," said Richard. "Try to steady yourself on the bits of rock that jut out," he added. "Find things to hold on to, and I'll get down slowly from the rock. Then, if I bend down, you can step on to it."

With the others gathered round, Richard did as he had said and soon Jackie and Jock were safely on the ground, with everyone talking at once and stroking the little dog.

Jackie put Jock down and he limped around them, whining with delight. She picked him up again. "I'll carry him home," Jackie said, adding: "Won't Arthur be pleased! You didn't tell him we were coming, did you, Jess?"

Jess shook her head. "I didn't want to raise his hopes," she explained. "It'll be a great surprise for him."

They set off back along the slippery rocks, hampered a little by their burden, which was handed from person to person.

"He gets to be quite a weight for such a little

dog, doesn't he?" commented Beckie, when it was her turn to carry Jock.

"He's all muscle!" said Jess.

Once they were back at the beach, it was a relatively uncomplicated journey back along the cliff path to where they had begun their search at the estuary. Columbus raced off across the reedy grassland above the mud-flats. He chased a seagull and then wheeled round in a wide circle, coming to a panting standstill in the reeds.

"It still looks very peaceful," Jess said, gazing around. "It's so lovely here, isn't it?"

"Mm. Nobody about, either. Even that fisherman's gone," agreed Beckie, standing beside her.

In the distance, Columbus was barking – short, sharp persistent barks.

"What is it, Col?" Richard called, shading his eyes from the sun. "What have you—" He stopped in mid-sentence, and the others heard his sharp intake of breath.

"What is it?" asked Rachel. Sam and Jackie, busy with Jock, turned their heads too.

When he spoke, Richard's voice was unusually low and quiet; frightened, even. "It's that fisherman," he said huskily, "he hasn't gone – look!"

Chapter 10

They all turned to look in the direction of Richard's pointing finger.

"But . . . it can't be . . ."

"He's . . . he's . . ."

It was Rachel who broke the spell. She spun round on the others. "Come on!" she said. "We mustn't just stand here. We must help him – quickly!"

"But . . . he's—" Even Sam was lost for words.

"He's sunk up to his armpits in mud," Rachel said tersely, "and if someone doesn't help him soon, he'll be drowned. The tide's coming in fast!"

Suddenly they shook off their inertia. Rachel was right. They must try to help – but how?

"We've got our rope," Richard said, "but . . . how do we get out there without sinking ourselves?"

"We ought to get help – the coastguards, or something," Beckie suggested.

"Yes, of course." Rachel looked at Jackie,

who was holding Jock tightly in her arms and looked frightened. "Jackie, could you do it? You're a fast runner. I remember hearing about you at school, from your brother."

"Where shall I go?" asked Jackie.

"The first house you can find," Jess told her, "there's a couple of cottages by the church. Ask to telephone the coastguard or the police. And an ambulance."

In a flash Jackie was gone, across the marshy ground, with Jock held tightly.

"I remember," Beckie said slowly, "reading about quicksand. You mustn't walk on it, but you lie down. Something like that. And that mud must be a bit like quicksand."

"That's right," joined in Richard. "You put something down on it – a coat or something like that."

"My sheet and rug!" added Jess triumphantly, pulling them out of her rucksack.

"So what's our plan?" asked Rachel.

"Go as far as we can without sinking," said Richard, "and then lay down the sheet and rug."

"And try to lasso him with the rope," finished Sam. "Let's go!"

Richard made Columbus wait on the path and they all set out towards the trapped fisherman, first across the reedy grassland and then over the mud. Gradually, the mud became more and more difficult to walk on without sinking in.

Rachel, slightly ahead of the others, stopped. "I don't think we dare go any further," she said. Jess looked back, and shivered. The land looked a long way off. "No, we mustn't," she agreed, "or we'll be in trouble, too."

Richard cupped his hands around his mouth. "Hello!" he shouted to the fisherman, "we're behind you, and we're going to try to help. We've sent for the coastguards. Don't move. Just lift your fingers, if you can, if you hear us."

Ahead of them the head and shoulders, its arms outstretched across the mud, remained as it had been, except that the fingers on the right hand moved slightly.

Richard shouted again. "We're going to try and send a rope over your head. If we make it, make sure that it goes *under* your arms. Then we'll try to pull you in."

"Sounds all right, doesn't it?" Richard muttered under his breath to his companions, as he tied a slip-knot to form the end of the rope into a noose. "But we're going to need a lot of luck."

"And we must act quickly," Jess reminded him, eyeing the water which, although quite a distance away, was lapping closer to the shore with each small wave. Jess laid the rug on the mud.

"We'll make a human chain," said Richard, "ankles to hands. Who will go first? I would, but I'd better not. I'm the heaviest, and besides I'm probably the strongest for pulling. Sorry, girls," he added with a wry smile.

"I'll go first," Beckie said, her voice determined.

"No, you mustn't, you won't be fit enough yet," Rachel said quickly. "I'll go. I'm nearly as light as you, and I'm probably stronger."

"No, Beckie returned. "I'm definitely the lightest."

"We haven't got time to argue," said Sam, her voice tense.

Beckie was already on the rug, crawling carefully across the covered mud, holding on to the sheet with one hand and gripping the rope in the other. When she reached the end of the rug she threw the sheet across the mud in front of her, moving cautiously. Then she crawled out again across the sheet, and Rachel crawled across the rug, followed by Sam.

Beckie wriggled as far off the sheet as she dared. Rachel held on to Beckie's ankles and behind her, Sam held hers, and Richard held Sam's.

"Right then, chain!" called Richard. "Have a go, Beckie."

From her half-kneeling, half-lying position, Beckie threw the coiled rope as hard as she could towards the half-submerged fisherman.

The rope fell short, but only a little way.

"I'll have to go further," Beckie said in a low voice over her shoulder to Rachel.

"Be careful," Rachel warned.

Beckie pulled in the rope, and re-coiled it. Then carefully she wriggled forward. She could feel the mud slopping around her waist and then the top of her legs. It slurped and clung to her like thick, brown, grasping tentacles, sucking, clutching . . . She lifted herself up with an effort and threw the rope. She could feel her body sinking, being sucked downward.

A shout came from behind her. "It's there," shouted Richard.

Beckie couldn't see. The effort of the throw

had made her body lurch forward, and she had been sucked in further. She could hear the mud all around her, sucking and slurping, moving and pulling.

"I mustn't let go," she thought to herself, wrapping the end of the rope around her hands, "it's his only chance. I mustn't let the rope slip through my hands."

Faintly, she could hear Richard's voice behind her, beyond the sound of the slurping mud. "I'm going to pull now. Hold on, everyone!"

It was like some horrible torture, Beckie decided, as she felt the pull on her ankles and then her shoulders as the rope tightened round her hands. For a moment she thought she would have to let go, as her body stretched. But she held on; fear filled her mind as the mud closed in around her, covering her eyes and seeping in through the sides of her mouth . . .

Beckie was being sick on the grass. All around her she could hear voices, and someone had a hand on her shoulder. "Hold on," said a voice – it sounded like Rachel, but she wasn't sure because her ears seemed to be full of mud. "I'm going to throw water over you," said the voice. The water followed, and at last she was able to open her eyes. It had felt like an eternity, but it had only been a couple of minutes since the pressure had suddenly eased and she had felt herself slipping and sliding back towards firmer ground, with the rope still taut in her hands.

It *was* Rachel. "Thanks," Beckie gasped, and grabbing the container she took a mouthful of the water. She swished it around her mouth before spitting it out. "Gosh, that's better." She sat up blinking and found herself looking into a frightened and extremely muddy face.

"Kevin! You were the fisherman!"

"Am I glad to see you lot!" replied the assistant Sparks, managing a weak smile. "I thought I'd had it!"

An ambulance had drawn up on the grass, and two ambulance-men were approaching gingerly across the firmer mud. Seeing the stretcher, Kevin began to stand up. "I don't need that," he began, but then his legs buckled under him.

"I think you probably do," said Richard.

Rachel looked across at Beckie. "And perhaps you ought to have a check up too," she said to her, "after all, it's not long since—"

"I'm fine," said Beckie firmly. "All I want now is a hot bath!"

Chapter 11

"You know Polly," Jess said, from her seat on the top bar of the orchard gate, "it's been a busy few days."

The gate was Jess's favourite place from which to talk to her pony, and Polly had grown accustomed to standing as still as a lively arab can whilst Jess continued. Polly even began to doze, for it was the end of the day; besides, she liked being tickled just behind her right ear.

"Yesterday was one of those days," Jess continued, leaning down to stroke the grey pony's neck with her free hand, "when all our problems seemed to come right – all at once!" Polly snorted, slowly and contentedly, and flicked a fly from her flank with a lazy swish of her tail.

"I was beginning to think we wouldn't find Jock for Arthur – and we did," Jess continued. "And then who would have thought that Kevin would be out on the mud-flats, fishing? He hadn't seen the notice – it had been blown

down in the wind – and he doesn't know the area. And we saved him, Polly girl!"

Polly's eyes were closing, sleepily.

"And Beckie was really brave, offering to take the front of the chain in the mud. It was quite dangerous, really. The coastguards told us off about it."

"But the best thing of all," Jess told her dozing pony, "is that Beckie and Rachel are friends now. Rachel thinks that Beckie was really brave, and it seems to have done Beckie good, somehow – given her more confidence. And Arthur," Jess went on, putting both her arms around her pony's neck, "was thrilled to bits to have Jock back – and he and Mrs Hasty seem to be getting on so well. Arthur's talking about giving up the filming business and settling down in the village. And you and I can put two and two together, can't we, Polly?"

Enough was enough, Polly decided. It was time to trot over to the other side of the field and join Muffin by the hedge. With a snort she pulled her head away and Jess slid off the gate, landing in the grass.

Watching the dapple-grey rump disappear into the dusk, Jess laughed with happiness.

Riding School

Three Girls, three ponies, three exciting adventures
by Samantha Alexander

Meet the pupils of Brook House Riding School . . .
Bound together by their passion for horses, three very
different girls – Jodie, Emma and Steph – each face a
thrilling challenge which tests their dedication to the limit.

Jodie is a talented rider who must find the courage to get
back in the saddle following a horrific traffic accident.

Emma has to prove her innocence when it appears her
carelessness has placed one of the riding school ponies in
danger.

Steph is shocked when she is dropped from the top riding
group. She recklessly turns her back on everything she
has been taught, and risks losing Monty her pony, for ever.

Other titles available from Macmillan and Pan Books

The prices shown below are correct at the time of going to press. However, Macmillan Publishers reserve the right to show new retail prices on covers which may differ from those previously advertised.